HEAVEN SENT

DELANEY DIAMOND

GARDEN AVENUE PRESS

1

Alejandro Sanchez crept through the dark room wearing boots, black clothes, and a black backpack on his back. Rain poured down in heavy sheets and lightning flashed outside the nearby window in a jagged line that illuminated the interior of the room. The rolling growl of thunder followed right after, so loud it rattled the windows and shook the foundation of the stone building.

He attached the last C-4 charge to the base of a load-bearing column. He had already placed explosives at key structural points in the stairwell, the basement, and specific areas of the foundation—all with the intent of destabilizing the massive structure and causing a collapse of the traffickers' lair. The extra internal placements would ensure nothing but rubble remained when he detonated the explosives. Fitting for a group of men who had destroyed so many lives, preying on young women in the nearby village and terrorizing their families to keep them in line.

Now to get the hell out of there.

He opened the door and moved swiftly but quietly through

the dark hall. Most of the men were asleep, but one or two wandered the halls and might see him if he wasn't careful.

As the thought crossed his mind, someone called to him from behind.

"Hey! Who are you?" the man demanded in Spanish.

These weren't the kind of men you talked to and reasoned with, so Alejandro didn't bother turning to face him. He took off and raced around a corner. Gunshots followed, splintering the wall near his head.

Mierda. That was way too close.

He stopped and removed the pistol from his holster. Flattening his back against the wall as much as he could with the backpack, he crouched low and lay in wait. When the man came into view, he shot up and into his face. The trafficker hit the far wall and crumbled to the floor, leaving a trail of blood in the paint.

The door at the end of the corridor flew open, and Alejandro sprang to his feet and ran in the opposite direction.

He tapped his earpiece. "This is Eagle One. Eagle Two, do you read me? Over."

The electronic device in his ear crackled, and then the Caribbean-accented voice of his colleague came through loud and clear.

"Eagle Two is here. Over." The voice belonged to Alissa.

"On my way. Over," Alejandro said, ducking down another hallway as automatic rounds splintered the wall.

Then the clanging sound of an alarm filled the air around him, and lights flashed like the strobe lights in a nightclub. He had to get out of there now. More men would be awake soon, and then he'd be in worse trouble.

"En route. Over," Alissa replied.

He could barely hear her because of the loud alarm.

He raced toward the large window at the end of the corridor and pointed his weapon at the glass. He pressed the trigger multiple times, and the glass shattered into pieces. Running full speed, he made a flying leap through the gaping hole and landed feet first on top of a truck cabin below.

The surface was wet and slick. He skidded and slipped off the top but landed on his feet, boots sinking into the muddy earth beneath him.

He made a quick turn toward the building, and as soon as the man appeared in the window, he discharged his weapon, hitting the man squarely in the chest. The round sliced through the guy's body, and he fell forward on top of the truck's cabin before rolling like a toppled log to the ground. Another man appeared in the opening, and Alejandro fired and missed. The guy shot back and missed before he rushed backward to hide in the shadowy darkness.

Alejandro fired two more times into the opening for good measure, breaking a piece of glass that fell in fragments to the ground. The extra shots should buy him time as the man continued to seek cover.

He sprinted across the property toward the trees. The dark and the rain made seeing difficult, but he plowed across the open field and into the brush, putting distance between him and the building. Crouching behind a large tree, he removed the remote detonator and pressed down with his thumb.

A loud *boom* filled the night air, followed by other thunderous *booms* in quick succession that rattled the trees and made the ground shudder. A black cloud of dust and debris reached toward the sky and was visible above the trees.

"*Adiós, pendejos,*" he said with satisfaction.

Alejandro darted deeper into the jungle. He had to get to the clearing on the other side, the extraction point where Alissa would pick him up.

Then he heard gunshots.

Goddamnit.

He figured once the alarm went off the men would be on

the alert, but he'd hoped he'd been able to kill them all. Wishful thinking. Some had managed to escape the building before the explosion.

Several rounds whizzed past him and cut holes in nearby trees. They were sweeping the brush with their automatic weapons in the hope of hitting him.

His heart galloped at a heightened rate as he zigzagged through the dense foliage, racing through the darkness across the slippery, treacherous terrain. He jumped over fallen tree trunks and tree roots and roughly brushed away branches that whipped toward his face. Raindrops pummeled the dense canopy of trees, and the nonstop downpour blurred his vision with a curtain of water.

He could hear his pursuers, so he couldn't slow down. They shouted at each other in Spanish as they came after him.

Alejandro ran harder, his breath coming out in ragged gasps. Determination gave him the energy he needed to keep moving.

Finally, he broke through the trees into the clearing. Straight ahead was the edge of a cliff, the dramatic drop below hidden by the dense fog hovering over the clearing.

"Eagle Two, where are you? Over."

"Thirty seconds out. Over."

"I need you here. Now."

The men's voices were coming closer. They were almost on top of him, and he was a sitting duck with nowhere to hide.

Alejandro swung toward the trees and lifted out his second weapon and pointed—feet planted in the muddy ground, his eyes swept the trees to anticipate where the men were coming from.

When the first criminal breached the trees, Alejandro fired, hitting him square in the chest and knocking him off his feet. Then he heard the beautiful sound of a helicopter's blades, and a rush of relief swamped him.

A black helicopter rose through the fog and darkness.

"Get down!" Alissa yelled in his ear.

Alejandro flung himself to the dirt and watched as the youngest member of their team sprayed the men breaking into the clearing. Mouse—tiny, light-skinned, with short-cropped hair—was in the back of the copter with an AK-47. The damn gun was almost as big as she was.

The distinctive crack of the powerful weapon filled the air, the bullets immediately piercing his pursuers' bodies. Three, four, then five men fell to the ground while another fell backward into the rain-soaked underbrush.

Alejandro shoved to his feet, but he was not out of danger yet. A truck was fast approaching. He made a split-second decision to pull a grenade off his tool belt.

"Come on! What are you doing?" Alissa demanded.

"Stay back," he replied.

The truck broke through the trees, and Alejandro faded left. He yanked the pin from the grenade and tossed it into the truck.

He heard the panicked cries of the men as he dropped to the mud again and covered the back of his head with his hands. The deafening roar of the explosion filled his ears. Metal, glass, and body parts shot into the air and landed all around him.

Alejandro lifted his head in time to see the shattered, inflamed truck careen over the edge of the cliff with a completely decimated truck bed.

Seconds later, Alissa landed the bird, and Alejandro hopped in. Brown-skinned, with her hair in cornrows, she shook her head.

"You couldn't help yourself, could you?" she asked.

Alejandro chuckled. "You know I like to blow things up."

He settled on the floor of the helicopter and removed a cigar from his pocket. It was soaking wet, so he simply stuck it in the corner of his mouth.

"Did you get them all?" Mouse asked.

"Hell yeah. They won't be bothering anyone else. We wiped them out." He grinned, and she gave him a high five.

Closing his eyes, Alejandro rested the back of his head against the helicopter and settled in for the ride to the airport. The waiting plane would take them out of the country—thanks to the local government that had hired them to eliminate the traffickers.

Another mission accomplished. And no one even knew they were in the country.

C amila Hughes strolled up to the register with a bag of Oreo cookies, cotton swabs, purple nail polish, and nail polish remover. Her toes were currently a mess, and she didn't have time for a pedicure before her brother's wedding tomorrow.

"How's it going, Julie?" she asked the cashier, placing her items on the counter.

"Same old, same old." Julie had frizzy-looking curly blonde hair braided into a big plait.

"I'll take this too." Camila tossed a pack of Tic Tacs on the counter.

Julie rang up the cookies. "Are you going to see Doug today?" she asked.

"How'd you guess—the cookies?"

"Yeah. I bet he loves you."

"Hopefully for more than free Oreos," Camila said with a laugh. "He called me two days ago and said he had something to show me. This is the first chance I've had free to talk to him, so I'm taking the Oreos as a peace offering to ask for his forgiveness."

"You're a good woman, Camila." Julie gave her the total and placed all the items in the bag.

"I try to be."

After Camila paid, she said goodbye and exited the drug store. Slipping a pair of Gucci sunglasses over her eyes, she walked to her custom-painted Volkswagen Beetle. Purple was her favorite color, and she owned way too many items in the color, including her vehicle. The paint job was an expensive splurge, but one that she didn't regret.

It was her trademark. Whenever people saw it, they knew she was somewhere in the vicinity doing what she did best—gathering local news for articles about everything Las Vegas had to offer—for the digital magazine, *Sin City Pulse*, often referred to as *The Pulse*. Some of the locals called her the "Blaxican chick" or the "Blaxican reporter" if they were feeling generous—an affectionate nod to her mixed-race heritage.

Camila slid behind the wheel, which she'd covered with a lavender and rhinestone wheel protector. She scooped her long, dark-brown hair into a ponytail holder and started the car. She'd make a quick trip to see Doug and then head to the airport to pick up Alejandro.

She brushed aside the anxiety the mere thought of his name evoked. He would only be in town for a couple of days to attend her brother's wedding. She could handle forty-eight hours in his presence.

She drove down Las Vegas Boulevard, famously known as the Las Vegas Strip. The city contained more meeting spaces than any other city in the country and was considered one of the world's top convention destinations, but Camila barely paid attention to the resorts and casinos lining the four-mile stretch of road. She'd lived there since she was ten years old. The glitz and dazzle that excited visitors no longer fazed her.

She drove into downtown Las Vegas, which most visitors never saw, where the homeless formed makeshift domiciles near malls and in parks. She'd spent a lot of time working with them and had not only earned their trust but considered many of them to be her friends. She was probably closest to Doug, an older white guy who'd been on the streets for over ten years.

His story was heartbreaking. A former veteran in his forties, he served multiple tours as an MP in Afghanistan before getting injured in a roadside bomb explosion. He was honorably discharged, but to this day couldn't lift his right arm at more than a forty-five-degree angle. They'd become close when Camila wrote a series of articles about the homeless population in Las Vegas and learned about his exploits as an investigator for the army.

She parked her vehicle at a plaza with low foot traffic. Every time she came here, she expected to see all the businesses gone because of the lack of customers and the lack of care the landlord took of the exterior. Trash littered the parking lot, and the building itself needed a new coat of paint—or at the very least, a pressure wash.

Camila removed her sunglasses, picked up the package of Oreo cookies from the car seat, and walked to the back of the building to a small homeless encampment. Men and women were huddled together with all their worldly possessions around them. They sat on worn cardboard mats and blankets as tattered and dingy as their clothes. Plastic bags, totes, and backpacks were stuffed to overflowing with their personal effects, some of which were stacked in shopping carts parked nearby.

Seeing them in these conditions broke her heart and angered her that more wasn't done to assist the over 600,000 people living on the street in the country. The country with the largest economy in the world should be able to provide shelter for all its citizens.

As she walked by, Camila called each familiar face by name and greeted them with a hand wave.

"Hey, Camila," they returned, some of their faces shadowed beneath hoodies and beanies, others covered with grime. The lines around their eyes and mouths indicated the hardship of living life on the streets, many of them looking decades older than their actual ages.

She went to the end but didn't see Doug anywhere. Finally, she retraced her steps and stopped in front of a woman sitting cross-legged on a folded blanket, her head covered with a faded green beanie.

Camila dropped to her haunches. "Hey, Rhonda, how's it going?"

"Doing okay. How about you, missy?" Rhonda asked in her raspy voice.

"Doing well. I have an article due on Monday, and my brother's getting married tonight."

"That's great news. Congratulations to him." Rhonda flashed a smile with missing teeth and sparkling eyes. Camila figured she must be close to Doug in age, but if she fixed her teeth and cleaned up, she could be quite attractive and take years off her appearance. Despite encouraging her to take advantage of the local services for people in her condition, Rhonda always declined, preferring to "keep to myself," as she put it.

But Camila suspected there might be another explanation. People ended up on the street for all kinds of reasons, such as medical bills, job loss, substance abuse, mental health issues. Early on, she noticed that except for Doug, Rhonda didn't let anyone touch her and suspected the older woman had ended up on the street because of some form of physical abuse.

"Have you seen Doug? He called me the other day, and I've been kinda busy, so this is the first chance I've had to catch up with him. I brought his favorite cookies."

Doug may have wanted to talk, but the most pressing reason for her visit was because he was leaving Las Vegas. He had often talked about his older sister, Melissa, and when Camila sensed he was ready to leave the streets, she offered to find his sibling. After initially declining, he agreed and gave as much information as he could, letting Camila know that, as of his last contact, his sister had been in San Diego.

Using her resources at the magazine, she had located his sister in less than a week, and the two siblings talked on the phone—which eventually led to Melissa inviting him to come live with her in San Diego. She had sent Camila money to buy him a prepaid cell phone so they could stay in touch and was driving in to get him on Sunday.

"I haven't seen Doug for a couple of days. This is his stuff right here." Rhonda tapped the mat beside her.

"That's weird. It's not like him to disappear for days, is it?" Camila had only known him a couple of years, but she couldn't remember him ever doing that before.

Rhonda shrugged. "I figured he was getting all gussied up for when his sister came."

She sounded a bit tart, and Camila could understand why. For a while she'd suspected the two were more than friends, and since Doug was leaving, she was probably hurt and bitter.

"Last I saw him, he was going down to the clinic on Eighth Street." That information came from an older Black man seated nearby—Sam. He sported a gray beard and friendly eyes, and his dark skin looked stretched paper thin.

"How do you know that?" Rhonda demanded.

"Cause he told me," Sam said, sounding defensive.

"Well, he didn't tell me," Rhonda said.

"You wasn't around. You was off somewhere—I don't know." He waved his hand dismissively.

"What about Poodle?" Camila asked. Doug had a dog that he treated like his own child.

"She's here," Rhonda answered.

On cue, a Jack Russell Terrier approached, wagging her tail.

"Hey, baby." Camila patted her head.

"Doug needs to hurry back. He didn't leave food for the dog. We've had to feed her the past two days, and it's not like we have a lot of extra food lying around," Rhonda grumbled.

"I'm sure Doug appreciates you taking care of his baby for him," Camila said.

Rhonda harrumphed, but Camila could tell she liked that Camila acknowledged her for taking care of Doug's pet.

"You can leave the Oreos with me," Rhonda said.

Camila hesitated. Not because she didn't trust Rhonda— there was a code among the homeless people. They looked out for each other. She hesitated because she'd hoped to see Doug *and* give him the bag of Oreo cookies, his favorite.

She handed over the cookies, careful to not make contact with Rhonda's hand. "Sam, did Doug say why he was going to the clinic?"

Sam screwed up his face in thought. "Nah. I figured maybe his stomach was bothering him again, I dunno."

"When was this?"

"Tuesday, I think." Three days ago. He must have been very ill to go to the clinic on a Tuesday.

Dr. Shapiro and his staff were generous with their time and labor. Years ago, they almost shut down, but an anonymous donor gave them the funding needed to stay open, and since then, they'd given back to the community in a selfless way. Dr. Shapiro had opened a clinic that provided hyperbaric oxygen therapy, treating all sorts of medical conditions, such as wound healing and sports injuries.

It was closed to the general public on Saturdays, but every second and fourth Saturday, they opened for half a day and accepted patients who otherwise couldn't pay—the homeless, impoverished, and prostitutes. As far as Camila was concerned, the doctor and his staff were angels for so generously donating their time.

"I hope he's okay. If either of you see Doug before I do, please let him know I'll be back tomorrow because I want to see him before he leaves. Rhonda, enjoy those cookies. I'll bring another pack when I stop by tomorrow."

"Bless you," Rhonda said effusively, tearing open the package.

Camila left the encampment and returned to her car, sitting for a moment in deep thought. It was strange that Doug had been gone for days and left his belongings and Poodle behind. And what had he called her about?

She dialed his number, but the call went straight to voice-mail. *He'll return soon enough*, she thought, starting the car. And he better not leave the city without saying goodbye.

She checked the time and then pulled out of the parking lot to head to the airport.

3

Camila pulled up outside the airport, her palms sweaty and her stomach a haven for butterflies. She sat in the car, watching passengers coming and going as she waited for Alejandro to arrive.

When he finally exited the building, the air stilled, and the world stopped spinning on its axis. She couldn't see his eyes behind the dark sunglasses, and his short-cropped hair was covered by a cowboy hat, but she recognized him immediately. She had known him too long not to.

He loved dark colors the same way she loved the color purple. He wore dark jeans and a black and gray muscle shirt that showed off his tattooed forearms and biceps. A brown duffel bag was thrown over one shoulder.

Several people—men and women—turned to stare at him, and she couldn't blame them. He was... eye-catching. Mesmerizing—his mestizo heritage blessing him with golden, tanned skin.

Her fingers tightened on her blinged out steering wheel as she held her breath, her heart thumping with each measured step he took along the sidewalk.

"Get out of the car," Camila whispered to herself.

At that very moment, Alejandro spotted her purple Beetle and paused, silently commanding her to get her ass out of the vehicle and come greet him. She took a deep breath, climbed out, and went up on the sidewalk, grinning and placing her hands on her round hips.

Alejandro approached slowly, leisurely, his walk as tantalizing as his appearance.

At almost 6'3, he was bulked up with muscles that displayed his strength and power. Tattoos crawled up the left side of his neck—two hissing snakes engulfed in flames. More tats covered his left arm, which she knew went all the way to his shoulder and across his left pec. His right arm was covered in tattoos up to his elbow.

His lips were a sculpted masterpiece, and for years, she'd fantasized about what they would feel like but had never had the pleasure of sampling them. At the moment, they appeared seductive with a roguish smile, but at other times, they hinted at a predatory ruthlessness he had acquired at a young age.

Why had she insisted he stay with her? He'd suggested staying in a hotel, but she had pointed out that she had an extra room since moving into her new place, and there was no need for him to spend the money. Privately, she believed she owed him. When her mother had died, he became her anchor, and his friendship had been invaluable.

They went back and forth until the argument became awkward and he finally gave in. Because she'd *insisted*. Now she wished she hadn't. She was definitely a glutton for punishment.

"Look at you," he said, stopping in front of her.

His voice was lethally seductive. Heavy and deeply masculine, accented with the endearing sound of rolled r's and a cadence that caused each word to flow with the warmth and rhythm of his native Spanish.

She couldn't see his eyes but by the tilt of his head knew that he looked her up and down. "Come here."

He didn't wait for her to move. He pulled her into a hug, and desire immediately dampened her panties. She winced but in the next breath happily squealed as he lifted her off the ground with one arm, crushing her soft breasts against his hard chest. His trimmed beard brushed against her cheek and tickled her skin.

When he finally placed her back on her feet, she breathed easier.

"Good to see you, *güey*," he said.

Camila hated when he called her that—*dude, buddy*—and grimaced internally. It meant he considered her one of the guys, and she wanted to be... more.

"Good to see you." She squeezed his biceps. "Have you gotten more muscular?"

"*Tal vez*," he said with a cocky grin.

Camila rolled her eyes. "How was your flight?"

"I cannot complain. I arrived safely." He wore several black necklaces and kissed the black cross pendant on one of them. "Thanks for coming to get me."

"Not a problem."

But having him in her home was going to be a problem. How the heck was she going to survive the next two days when her panties were already wet from a simple hug?

"I can't believe you still have this thing." Alejandro eyed the car.

"Why do you hate my baby so much?"

"It's an attention getter. You cannot be incognito in a purple vehicle everybody knows you own."

She shrugged. "I like being known. I'm not an FBI agent like you."

"I am not an FBI agent."

He'd never told her about his work for the government organization that had trained him as a young man. She didn't even know its name. Now he worked for The Cordoba Agency, a company that provided investigative and bodyguard services. As far as she was concerned, he might as well be FBI. She worried about him and the work he did but took comfort in knowing he was good at his job.

"Put your bag in the back." Camila hit the key fob, and the trunk opened. While he placed his bag inside, she slid behind the wheel.

Seconds later, Alejandro joined her. Because of his size, everything else shrunk in comparison, and her car suddenly felt way too small for the two of them.

He pushed back the seat to accommodate his long legs.

"Good?" she asked, starting the engine.

"Good," he confirmed.

She checked the mirrors and then slowly pulled away from the curb.

Alejandro clapped his hands together. "So what's the plan? How much trouble are we getting into tonight?"

"Not too much. Miguel and Patrice are having a combined bachelor and bachelorette party, so you'll have to be on your best behavior, and thankfully, you won't be able to get my brother into any trouble."

Alejandro groaned and muttered a curse.

"Sorry." Camila shrugged, though she was anything but sorry.

"I guess I'll have to behave myself," he muttered. "So, tell me what you've been up to."

They didn't talk as much as they used to, and the last time they saw each other was over a year ago when he came for her mother's funeral.

"I've been working on new articles for *Sin City Pulse*. The owner allowed me to write a few hard-hitting pieces, including a whole series on the homeless situation in Las Vegas. He wants me to do more features like that."

"More than the usual *Top Ten Must-See Attractions in Vegas* pieces?" he teased.

"Yes, more than that."

Camila smiled briefly. Alejandro had a great sense of humor, but most people didn't see that side of him. It was reserved for the people closest to him. She knew the complexity of the man he was. Everyone else saw a tough guy with a mean, take-no-shit face, but it didn't detract from his attractiveness, which was multiplied when he dared smile.

"Not too long ago, he asked if I'd be interested in taking over the website," Camila continued.

"Would you do that?" he asked, sounding surprised.

She flicked on her indicator to go around a slow-moving car. "I thought long and hard about the offer and realized I do *not* want the responsibility. I'm pretty happy doing what I do, earning a base salary and a percentage of the ad revenue, without the headache of responsibility he has. If he wasn't so candid about the problems with the other writers, IT, et cetera, I might have accepted his offer. However, I have zero interest in taking over for him."

"Sounds like he shot himself in the foot," Alejandro said.

She laughed softly. "He did. Have you had any interesting assignments lately?"

"No. I've mostly been doing paperwork and working a few local bodyguard assignments. Temporary jobs. Nothing major."

"Or dangerous?" Camila asked.

"Or dangerous," he confirmed, though she didn't quite believe him. "Little Miguel is getting married. I can't believe it," Alejandro said with a shake of his head.

At twenty-eight, Miguel was five years younger than Camila. They had both been born in LA before the family moved to Las

Vegas. Their mother was from Mexico and their father African-American, and they spent summers with their maternal grand-mother in a small town in the state of Jalisco. As kids, Miguel tried to follow Camila, Alejandro, and Emilio—their other good friend—around, but they always shooed him away and made him play with the kids his age.

"He's not so little anymore, but I can't believe it either. And he actually got someone to agree to marry him!" Camila slowed to a stop at a red light.

"He is a good guy, and earning his PhD is a big deal. I'm sorry I missed his hooding ceremony."

"He understood you're a busy man—protecting clients, saving the world."

Alejandro let out a soft, sexy chuckle that made her nipples tighten. Everything he did was sexy.

"I am not saving the world. Trust me," he said.

Again, she didn't quite believe him.

After a few more minutes, they arrived at the two-bedroom house she rented in a small community with a pool, tennis courts, and walking trails. She pulled under the carport and led the way inside.

"This is my humble abode," she announced, tossing the keys on the counter. "As you can see, it's nicer than the one-bedroom apartment I used to live in."

Coming in through the carport, they entered the dining room/living room combination and faced the small kitchen separated by a bar. A big, comfy looking purple sofa and two purple and pearl-gray armchairs were in the living room area facing a television mounted on the wall. The white walls were mostly empty, except for a few family photos, including a picture of her as a young girl with her grandmother in Jalisco.

"Very nice," he remarked.

"It's okay. I haven't done much decorating, but it's home, for now."

"For now?"

Camila shrugged. "I don't know how long I'll stay in Vegas. I'm getting restless, I guess. Miguel is getting married, and Mommy and Daddy are gone." Her husband was gone too. There was no reason for her to stay.

"What about the house? Have you sold it?" He asked the words gently, carefully.

Probably because he knew her parents' death was a sensitive topic for her. She did her best to hide how much losing them had affected her, but losing loving parents was difficult for anyone, and she and her parents had been particularly close. She truly hadn't fully recovered from first her father's death from leukemia, then her mother's unexpected heart failure two years later on the anniversary of his death.

She shook her head as pain sliced through her. "The house is still there, empty. I pay a cleaning service to go in once a month, but other than that, I can't bring myself to box up their things, and I can't bring myself to sell the house. I grew up there. We had so many meals and parties and celebrations there. Too many memories."

"Do you know where you want to live, if you move?" Alejandro asked.

Camila blew out a breath. "Not yet. Still deciding. Maybe I'll move back to LA. Who knows? Let me show you to your room."

She led Alejandro down the short white hall. "This is the bathroom," she said, shoving open the first door to the left. She continued down the hall. "This is where you'll sleep, and my room is at the end." She pointed at the closed door.

Alejandro entered the guest room, a small, sparsely furnished room with a dresser and a queen bed large enough to accommodate his big body. Floral print sheets and a light-weight green blanket covered the bed.

"Thanks, this is nice." He tossed his duffel bag on the floor.

"Much better than sleeping under the stars, right?" Camila asked with a grin.

He frowned in confusion, then a faint smile touched his lips as he remembered. They were twelve and thirteen when the two of them were out at night, talking about their dreams. She had told him he had to come to the United States one day to see her. He had listened to her tell him stories and admitted he dreamed of visiting Las Vegas, but he lived with his grandmother, and they didn't have a lot of extra money—certainly not for traveling.

Staring up at the black sky, they had fallen asleep on the grass, only awakening when *her* grandmother found them and sent Alejandro home.

She had glared down at them. *"Xochitl Camila,"* she had said, fists on her ample hips, calling her by her first name—the name of her Aztec ancestors.

Her indigenous grandfather had given her the name, which meant "flower" in the Nahuatl language and symbolized grace and natural splendor. She went by Camila because most people, including Mexicans, couldn't pronounce her name correctly. Alejandro had learned to pronounce her name properly, and she had always appreciated the effort.

"Señora Carrizosa was *not* happy. I was worried she'd cut you off from me," he said.

"We weren't doing anything wrong, so I knew she wouldn't, but staying out that late, when she didn't know where I was, was not a good idea. Well, I have some work to finish, an article, so I'll have tonight and tomorrow to devote to the happy couple. Do you need anything?"

"I'm fine."

"If you do need anything, help yourself," Camila said. "There's plenty of food and drinks and beer in the fridge. *Mi casa es su casa.*"

"Gracias."

She paused on her way out. "I'm glad you came, Alejandro. It's good to see you."

"It's good to see you too." He tilted his head to the side, concern in his eyes. "*¿Estás bien?*"

She smiled briefly. "Yes, I'm fine."

She left him alone, and the familiar heaviness in her lower belly appeared, a reminder of long held regrets.

4

Alejandro straightened the collar on his black shirt and stepped back from the mirror. He had left the top two buttons undone to show off his chains. There were four of them, black and granite silver, of different lengths and designs. One held a cross pendant, given to him by his grandmother for protection. The other held a black onyx ring, one of the few possessions he had left from his father.

He stepped out of the room and found Camila standing by the bar that separated the kitchen from the rest of the front of the house, rummaging through a little black purse. Almost immediately his body hummed to life, and he almost swallowed his tongue.

Every time he saw her, it was impossible to look away. When she was younger, she wore her hair curly, but nowadays mostly wore it straight and pulled away from her elegant round features. Not tonight. Tonight, her hair was styled in loose chocolate waves that tumbled to the middle of her back. She was a stunning woman—with womanly curves and D-cup breasts he longed to stroke with his tongue.

She had donned a little purple dress with gold straps, and

black slingback heels showed off the arch in her calves. A familiar ache twisted through his balls, which for years he'd fought to diminish by bedding other women, but he was always left wanting because they weren't her.

Camila looked up as he approached, a smile taking over her face as she did a quick sweep of him from top to bottom.

Her sun-kissed skin was the palest brown, and her sultry eyes sparkled, radiating warmth and mischief. Her lips were ruby-red, and her sweet smile held a teasing edge, as if she knew the effect her beauty and charm had on people and liked to play with it.

"Ready?" she asked.

"Let's go," Alejandro said.

The strip at night was a dazzling spectacle of bright lights and energy, transformed into a setting that highlighted the glamor and excess of the city. Neon signs and huge LED billboards illuminated the entire length of the boulevard with their glow.

The towering casinos—such as the Bellagio, with its iconic dancing fountains, and the pyramid-shaped Luxor—promoted their shows with flashing advertisements. People from all over the United States and the world crowded the sidewalks, stopping to snap photos with street performers or take a detour into one of the bars and restaurants that advertised delicious-looking meals.

The combined bachelor and bachelorette party was taking place at the Celestial Palace Hotel and Casino, a newly renovated establishment on the strip. When they arrived, Alejandro stepped out of Camila's car and waited while the valet took her keys. They walked into the glittering interior together, his ears filling with the sounds of slot machines and the murmur of voices. The air was electric, with all manner of guests roaming around, sitting at the slots, or playing at one of the tables.

The high ceiling was painted with the image of cherubs and

harp-playing angels and dotted with large, shimmering chandeliers. Sleek, high-end furnishings in deep blues and rich golds added a luxurious touch.

"So, here's the agenda for the night," Camila began. "Dinner first, we attend the ceremony, and then we come back to celebrate at the club, where Miguel and Patrice have a VIP section for us."

"Sounds good."

He had downplayed his activities when Camila asked what he'd been up to, but after his last assignment in South America, where he and the team had saved those young women from being trafficked, he was looking forward to partying.

When they entered the restaurant, he fell back so Camila could talk to the hostess. He took that opportunity to capture every detail of her appearance, conducting a visual tour of her petite frame, all the way down to the curve in her waist and the flare of her hips.

Being with Camila was both pleasure and pain. He enjoyed spending time with his friend, but it was torture. He wanted her, and there were times when he thought he saw the same want in her eyes. But even if he did, he couldn't act on it. He wasn't a scumbag. Camila was off-limits. Not only because they were friends, but because she was his best friend's widow.

They followed the hostess into the dining area, where the lights were dimmer, and the walls filled with art depicting abstract designs and scenes from the city's nightlife. Bars with glass countertops and mirrored backs reflected the lights, with guests crowded around them drinking colorful drinks.

As soon as Miguel saw them, he hopped up from the table. Lean, with obviously freshly cut curls, he wore a suit and tie and a pair of black-framed glasses.

"Alejandro, *hermano*! So glad you could make it."

Alejandro pulled him into a hug, and they patted each

other on the back. "Of course. I would not have missed this for the world."

Miguel stepped back and extended his hand toward a young woman who came to her feet behind him. "This is Patrice, my future bride—the woman who tamed me."

Alejandro smiled. Miguel had never been wild. Camila had been the wild, reckless one while he had always been studious and careful. It didn't help that he was younger, so Camila always wanted to protect him, as any older sibling would.

His fiancée extended a hand to Alejandro. "Nice to meet you. I've heard a lot about you."

"Nice to meet you too."

Patrice was short and thick and wore a bridal veil and hot pink mini-dress that hugged her voluptuous curves. Her caramel-toned face was blemish-free except for a small mole on her left cheek.

There were six more people at the table—three men and three women. Introductions were made, and then Alejandro and Camila sat across from each other.

Miguel and Patrice had selected a family-style menu for the group. Once everyone was seated, the two waitresses assigned to their table brought out their drink orders and the appetizers.

"What did you do today?" Alejandro asked, stabbing his calamari with a fork.

"Yesterday we went sightseeing, and today we rode ATVs through the desert," Miguel answered.

"That was this morning. Then we relaxed by the pool until it was time to get ready for dinner," Patrice added.

"I've been looking forward to a vacation, and this was perfect," said Kia, a friend of Patrice's. She had spiky blonde hair and an edgy look.

"What about you?" Miguel asked Alejandro.

Camila answered for him. "Remember I told you, he flew in

this afternoon. He hasn't had a chance to do much of anything except rest and get ready for tonight."

"Oh right. Did you finish your article?" Miguel asked.

Camila nodded. "I'll let the piece marinate and then review it one more time tomorrow before I send the file to Adrian."

Miguel sipped his drink, a light frown furrowing his brow. "You seem off, sis. What's wrong?"

"Do I?" Camila let out an obviously forced laugh. "It's silly, but I'm a little worried about a friend of mine," she admitted.

"Who?" Miguel slipped his arm across the back of his fiancée's chair.

"Doug—the homeless guy whose sister I found. No one has seen him in a while, and the last person who talked to him said he was going to the clinic."

Alejandro had sensed something was off with her earlier, and now he knew he was right. She was worried about her friend. He respected her relationship with the unhoused population in the city. From a child, she'd always been passionate about helping people who lived on the street. In Jalisco, she had worked closely with the church to feed and clothe the homeless, so it was no surprise that as an adult she championed the same cause.

"He's probably fine," Miguel said.

"I wish I knew for sure. He called me, but when I called him back, he didn't answer. He always answers his phone." Camila sighed. "Ignore me. I'm sure he'll turn up. His sister arrives on Sunday, and I know he doesn't want to miss her."

The smile on her lips wavered, then disappeared. She suddenly looked lost. She obviously didn't believe what she said. That was the problem with Camila. She felt too much. She wouldn't be satisfied until she knew for sure this Doug guy was okay.

"It will be okay." Alejandro mouthed the words across the

table to her, and she smiled gratefully at his effort to put her mind at ease.

The conversation shifted, and soon the group was laughing and teasing each other. Camila told a few funny, embarrassing stories about Miguel, and Kia told a couple about Patrice. The time flew by quickly as they enjoyed themselves, and soon it was time to head to the chapel.

They climbed into a party bus with U-shaped plush leather seating, the interior illuminated by color-changing LED lights and a spinning disco ball suspended from the mirrored ceiling. In the middle was a chrome dance pole Kia took full advantage of, dancing to a bumping hip-hop beat while the group egged her on.

Alejandro sat in the back and watched with his arms resting atop the seat. He enjoyed watching women dance, but the only person he wanted to see gyrate tonight was Camila. His gaze met hers once, and she inclined her head toward the pole and arched an eyebrow, indicating he should give the group a dance. He signaled his displeasure with narrowed his eyes, and a peal of laughter burst from her lips, the beautiful sound carrying the short distance between them and causing a twist of longing in his gut.

The chauffeur took them to the chapel where an officiant waited. Patrice and Miguel wanted to be married at ten-thirty-six because that was the time they'd met on campus at a student party five years ago.

Inside, the eight guests watched the couple exchange vows and rings, and Alejandro shot a surreptitious glance at Camila. Despite the many women he'd slept with over the years, he had never considered marrying any of them. The only woman he would have considered marrying, Camila, had been out of reach. From the moment she and Emilio became a couple, jealousy had eaten through him—that his friend had been lucky enough to capture this magnetic, vivacious creature and call her his own.

The officiant waited until exactly ten-thirty-six before he said the words they'd all been ready to hear: "I now pronounce you husband and wife. You may kiss your bride."

Miguel kissed his wife and dipped her over his arm to the whooping and hollering of their friends. Camila shot Alejandro a pleased look, and he smiled back. But the night was not over.

"Time to party!" Miguel yelled.

With excited cries from all the women, they left the chapel and climbed into the waiting party bus, which returned them to the Celestial Palace. They made their way to the VIP section of The Firmament, the Palace's popular nightclub. The group of ten gathered together on the soft leather seats, and waitresses brought out champagne, cake, and more food for them.

"To the happy couple! May you have many, many, many happy years together!" Camila stood in the middle of the group, holding up a flute with the golden liquid.

"Amen!"

"Here, here!"

Everyone touched their glasses together and then sipped the flavorful drink.

Camila sank onto her chair, eyeing the spread of heavy hors d'oeuvres before them. She clutched her stomach. "If I eat anything else, I'm going to explode."

"Same," Patrice laughed, seated on Miguel's lap. She was glowing, her rings sparkling on her finger.

"We need to dance off the food and dance off this energy," Kia suggested.

She jumped up and hauled Patrice and Camila with her, both of them groaning and dragging reluctantly behind. Two of the guys followed while the third male and the other female slinked off to a corner to be alone.

Alejandro changed seats and sat down next to Miguel. From this vantage point, he had a good view of the dance floor and watched Camila shaking her hips with her hands in the air. One of the guys in their group—lanky with coffee-hued skin, sidled up behind her, and Alejandro's jaw tightened. His whole body became rigid. He couldn't blame the guy. She was sexy, beautiful, captivating. But that didn't mean he didn't want to bash his face in.

Miguel leaned toward him. "Camila won't say it, but she misses you. You should call more often, and you shouldn't stay away so long."

"Has it been long?" Alejandro lit a cigar. Leaning back, legs spread, he never let his eyes drift from Camila and her dance partner. He had inconveniently forgotten the sexual heat that plagued him in her presence, forcing him to act cool while he burned on the inside.

"She hasn't seen you since you came to Mommy's funeral," Miguel reminded him.

Alejandro knew that. Over a year had passed. "Too long," he admitted in a low voice.

But how could he explain the reason for his absence? The guilt he felt for wanting Camila while knowing nothing would ever happen. Not with the ghost of Emilio between them. Not knowing when given the choice, she had chosen Emilio over him.

5

Kia sidled up to Camila at the bar.

"I have a bone to pick with you. I can't believe *that's* Alejandro, your good friend. Damn. Does he have a girlfriend?"

Camila tipped the club soda to her lips and took a drag before answering. "No."

"So he's fair game?" Kia arched a blonde eyebrow.

Camila froze. "What do you mean?"

Resting a hand on her narrow hip, the blonde shot a glance in the direction of the VIP section. "I'm thinking about taking a shot at him before Lydia does," she said, referring to the other single woman in their group.

Straightening, Camila cleared her throat as an ugly emotion burned in her stomach. "Both of you would be fools to hit on him."

"Why? Because he's not the relationship type? I just want to get my back blown out, and he looks like a back blower."

Camila couldn't deny that. She'd often wondered about his sexual prowess herself. Kia actually licked her lips, and Camila gripped the glass bottle so she wouldn't be tempted to smash it over her head.

"Bad idea," she said.

"Why?"

Camila dropped her voice to a conspiratorial level, leaning toward Kia so she could be heard above the loud music and revelry. "I shouldn't tell his business, but Alejandro is secretly in love with another man. He's gay."

Kia's mouth fell open. She stared at Alejandro for a moment before she returned her gaze to Camila. "*Really*?"

Camila shrugged. "Gay men come in all shapes and sizes. You know that," she said, referring to Kia's cousin, who was gay.

"Yeah, you're right, but Patrice never mentioned he was gay."

"A lot of people don't know, and... I've said too much and betrayed his confidence." She hoped she looked contrite.

"Well, I know you two are close. You've known each other since you were kids, right?"

"That's right."

"And he's always been that way?"

"For as long as I've known him."

Kia's brow wrinkled. "You're sure he's not bisexual?"

Camila pursed her lips regretfully. "He's not. He only swings one way, and that's gay."

Kia let out an exaggerated sigh. "There goes my plans for a weekend hookup."

Camila patted her arm. She felt a little guilty, but the thought of Kia and Alejandro together made her nauseous. The thought of Alejandro and any woman together made her nauseous. She remembered the first time he'd introduced her to one of his girlfriends back in Jalisco. For two days she had stayed indoors, claiming to have a stomach virus so she wouldn't have to see him.

Right now he was smoking a cigar while talking to her

brother. He had rolled up the sleeves on his black shirt, and they gripped his veiny forearms covered in hair and tattoos. His powerful thighs, clad in dark-gray slacks, were set apart, and the unbuttoned top of his shirt revealed hair on his chest and his collection of chains. He was easily the hottest man in the club, oozing sex appeal and virility with minimal effort.

Camila greedily gulped her water to cool off.

The wedding guest she had been dancing with earlier came up to them. "Can I entice you ladies back onto the dance floor?" he asked, shaking his shoulders.

She pushed away from the bar and set a regretful smile on her lips. "I'm tired, and I'm going back to the VIP. You two have fun."

She ignored his disappointed expression and headed toward Alejandro and Miguel. She climbed the stairs to the VIP and plopped down beside Alejandro.

"What are you two talking about?" she asked.

Miguel turned bloodshot eyes toward her. He'd clearly had his share of drinks. "Alejandro is giving me life advice like a good brother should."

"Are you going to take the advice and apply it?" Camila asked.

"Of course! Right now, however, I see someone is bothering my wife, and I can't put up with that shit." He removed his glasses and pushed up from the chair.

"Please don't start a fight," Camila called after him.

He waved her off and stumbled toward the dance floor.

"Oh lord, I have a bad feeling that now he has a few drinks in him, he's going to act like some macho guy. I'd hate for Patrice to see him get his butt kicked," Camila said.

"Don't worry, I won't let him get into trouble tonight," Alejandro said, amusement tilting up the corners of his mouth.

"Thank you," she said with a short laugh.

Camila watched him take a puff of his cigar, its leathery

scent circulating around them and curling into her lungs. She removed it from his hand, and he looked at her in surprise.

"Cohiba?" she asked.

"Of course."

She brought the cigar to her lips, experiencing a thrill that *his* lips had seconds before been in the same place. She took a puff, and the subtle sweetness from the wrapper coated her tongue, mixed with the taste of spices.

She took another puff and released in a deliberate, controlled blow, letting the smoke wind in a snakelike manner toward the ceiling.

"Can I have my cigar back now?" Alejandro asked.

Smirking, she glanced at him through the veil of smoke. She enjoyed the earthy taste that lingered on her tongue and took another puff before handing him the Cohiba.

"Nice," she said.

She felt relaxed and a bit naughty. Maybe because she was smoking after him, or maybe it was the drinks she'd downed throughout the night. Whatever the reason, she wasn't herself. She felt fearless. Reckless. Horny from the dull throb between her thighs.

She crossed her legs, and Alejandro's eyes shifted to where the short hem of her dress rode up on her thigh.

"Are you having a good time?" Camila asked.

He lifted his dark eyes to meet hers, but his expression remained unreadable. She wished she knew what he was thinking.

"I am. Are you?"

She nodded. "I needed to get out and have fun more than I realized."

"Me too. It's a reminder that everyone needs down time." He took a drag on the cigar and handed it back to her.

She took a puff and then returned it. "You should stay in town longer. You work a lot. I know you have vacation accrued."

"I do, but I'm going to Jalisco when I leave here. I have not been to my parents' graves in a long time. I need to go and check on them."

Camila was disappointed but understood. Unlike her, Alejandro didn't have much close family. She had a brother and cousins and aunts and uncles on both sides, all of whom she had a great relationship with. But he only had his maternal grandmother. He had lost his parents at a young age and went to live with her, whom he called Mamita, which was how she and he met. Her grandmother and his grandmother had attended the same church, where Emilio's father was the priest.

People in town had said Alejandro had demon's blood running through his veins, but she never cared who he was, though all the adults knew. He was the son of Carmen and Luis Sanchez, career criminals who had ruled the town they lived in. Carmen died in a knife fight with another woman, and Luis passed when he crossed the wrong dirty cop. When his father died, Alejandro had only been eleven years old and was immediately shipped off to the town where his grandmother lived.

"I told Kia that you're gay," Camila blurted.

Alejandro cocked his head and looked at her as if she'd grown a second nose. "What?"

"I told Kia that you're gay." She shrugged.

"I heard you. Why the hell did you tell her that?" he demanded, sounding confused.

"I don't know." She did know, but she couldn't tell him.

"Out of the blue, you tell a woman who I do not know that I am gay?"

"She wanted a weekend fling, and that's why I said what I said."

His eyes filled with disbelief as he studied her. "You messed up my chance to get laid this weekend?"

"You can get laid whenever you want, Alejandro. I'm sure

you have plenty of women in Hopevale falling all over you."
She sniffed, angling away from him.

Hopevale was a town not far from Atlanta, Georgia where
he had settled.

"I do not."

"I don't believe you," Camila said, hoping the jealousy
didn't seep through her voice.

"It is the truth, whether you believe me or not."

She crossed her arms over her chest, purposely pushing her
breasts higher. She experienced a modicum of satisfaction
when his eyes flickered to her bosom for a second.

She finally asked the question she'd been dying to know.
"You don't have a girlfriend in Georgia—some nice Southern
belle cooking you heaping bowls full of shrimp and grits and
all kinds of Southern dishes?"

The intensity of his stare burned the side of her face, but
she refused to look at him.

"Most of the time, I cook for myself. Sometimes I go to
Sunday dinner at my boss's house. Other times, I eat out. I
cannot remember the last time a woman cooked for me, but if
she did, I'd rather have *camarones embarazados* served with a big
bowl of *frijoles charros* on the side."

Camila shot him a glance from the corner of her eye. "If you
were staying longer, I could make that exact meal for you."

She had spent a lot of time in the kitchen with her grandmother during the summers and had fond memories of
learning to make traditional Jalisco dishes.

"You might make me stay longer than planned," he
drawled.

Camila's heart thumped faster in her chest, heat spreading
over her exposed neck and arms. She hadn't cooked for him in
years. Not since Emilio was alive.

"Do you know who he is? He looks important." Alejandro
squinted through spiraling smoke, and Camila followed his

gaze to a group of men walking toward a different VIP section. A mid-forties, Andy Garcia look-alike in a beige suit and black tie was flanked on either side by four men who towered over him.

Camila smirked. "So, I was right? You really are gay?"

Alejandro blew smoke out the corner of his mouth while his eyes did a slow tour of her body. "We both know I'm not gay, but if you need me to prove it..."

Her breath hitched and heat—burning heat—washed over her and made her pulse dance. His behavior threw her for a loop. She couldn't recall him ever looking at her like that before and didn't know how to react. She decided that answering his question was safer.

"That's Javier Reyes. He's a billionaire. He owns this casino and several others. One he's renovating here and two in Macau. His office is at the top of this building. He's not a nice guy."

"I guess that's why he needs those bodyguards," Alejandro murmured. He rested his wrist on his thigh, his attention focused on Reyes and his men.

"A lot of the casinos aren't owned by the same people who own the buildings, but in his case, he owns both. He took over when his father retired. Word is that Javier is a control freak and ten times worse than his father. His name has been linked with shady business practices, bribery, even burying people alive in the desert as some kind of sick punishment. No surprise, the cops are in his pocket, which means he does whatever the hell he wants. He basically acts as if he's a gangster instead of a businessman and has a huge compound thirty-five minutes outside of Vegas. Apparently, he contributed quite a bit to its design, so he's really proud of it. The compound is supposedly guarded by a small army of security. He throws the occasional party, and from what I understand, they're pretty wild."

"You never received an invitation?" Alejandro asked in a teasing voice.

"I wouldn't accept if I did. I would normally never spend a minute in any of his establishments, but Miguel and Patrice received a good deal on the casino's wedding package, so here we are."

The biggest bodyguard, a Black man dressed in a black suit, yanked a man from his seat in the VIP.

"Oh boy, I wonder what he did," Camila whispered.

The bodyguard gripped the man's arm and hauled him out of the section, and the others followed. She couldn't hear what he was saying, but it was obvious the man was pleading. It was strange to see everyone continuing to dance and party, as if a man wasn't being dragged through the club.

As they passed by, Javier turned his head in Alejandro and Camila's direction, and a shiver traveled up her spine when his eyes met hers. Something about him sent fear tunneling through her, and she dropped her gaze. Alejandro, however, continued to look at them until they left.

"Do you know him?" he asked.

"I've never met him before in my life." Feeling a sudden chill, she wrapped her arms around herself. "What do you think is going to happen to the man they took?" she asked, though she had a good idea.

"If what you said about Reyes is true, my gut says he's a dead man."

6

"We'll see you tomorrow."

Alejandro watched as Camila and Miguel hugged warmly.

"Congratulations again, *hermanito*. You're both lucky to have found each other." Camila kissed her brother's cheek.

"I wish Mommy and Daddy could have been here," Miguel said wistfully, his speech slurred.

"They are. Right here," Camila assured him, placing her palm over his chest.

Miguel beamed at Alejandro over her head. "You see why I love this woman right here? She's the best sister in the world." He flung his arm around Camila's neck and squeezed her tight to him.

They and the rest of the wedding party spent a few more minutes talking, and then there were hugs all around. Finally, Alejandro and Camila left the group, who wanted to stay behind to continue partying.

"Are we old?" she asked with a laugh as they walked through the casino.

"I think so. They'll probably be up until morning while

we'll be fast asleep. I'm driving, by the way. You have had enough to drink tonight."

"I'm not drunk, but I'm not going to argue with you. I'm tired." She scowled at him but handed over the valet ticket.

They didn't have to wait long before the valet brought her purple car to the front, and they climbed in.

"You look great behind the wheel of my baby. Lavender and rhinestones suit you," Camila teased.

"I'm secure enough in my manhood to appreciate that compliment," Alejandro said, with exaggerated seriousness.

She laughed and rested her head against the seat.

The ride back to her house was completed in silence. Each time Alejandro looked at her, she had her eyes closed, her deliciously round breasts rising and falling as she breathed softly.

He wondered if he should stay longer. Camila was right, he had plenty of vacation time available. He'd sleep on it and make a decision in the morning.

When he arrived at her house, he pulled under the carport and put the car in park. The neighbors' houses were dark, and all around them the night was quiet, except for the distant sound of traffic going by on the main road.

"Camila?"

"Hmm? I'm not sleeping." She turned her head, giving him a heavy-lidded look between her lashes.

"You need to go to bed. It's been a long day," Alejandro said, though sleeping was the last thing on *his* mind.

He wanted to kiss her ruby-red lips and sink his fingers into her silky hair while she rode his dick. Panting, begging him for more. He'd never been more tempted by the urge to kiss her. How did someone manage to look so delectably sexy while drowsy?

He ran a hand down his face. The fantasies had become graphic in the short time he had been there. Decision made. No need to wait until tomorrow. He was getting the hell out of

Dodge on Sunday as planned, or he'd end up doing something he regretted.

Camila groaned. "I'm coming, I'm coming."

They climbed out of the vehicle, and he opened the door to the house and let them inside. "Go to bed. I'll lock up."

"Thank you." She flung her arms around his torso and rested her cheek to his chest. "You're a good friend, Alejandro. Good night."

She raised up on her toes and gave him a quick kiss on the cheek. The soft touch landed on his skin with the explosive power of a detonated grenade. Then she walked down the hall, leaving him to look after her with a semi-hard penis and a clenched fist.

"Good friend. Yeah, that's me," he mumbled.

As he told her he would, he checked the windows and the doors, frowning at the flimsy lock on the door leading from the carport. He'd replace it before he left. He peered out the kitchen window at the night. Everything looked calm and peaceful.

Satisfied, he went into his bedroom and stripped off his clothes, changing into loose-fitting sleep shorts. He tightened the drawstring and then removed a bottle of pills from his bag. He tapped one of the multi-vitamin tablets into his palm and made his way to the kitchen and poured himself a glass of water.

Sitting on the sofa, he tossed back the water and swallowed the pill. Lying on his back, he absentmindedly rubbed the spot where an empty ache settled in his chest.

He stared up at the ceiling and thought about his relationship with Camila. Violence had been a part of his life from a young age. He met her when he was a sullen, angry eleven-year-old whose mother was dead and whose father had been shot down in the street like a dog. Instead of fearing him, she approached and said, "*Hola*." Then she smiled and handed him a flower, the same bright reddish-orange as the one tucked into the curls behind her ear.

He had believed, because his parents had done horrible things, he too would become a horrible person. Yet she saw something different in him.

From that moment, he had wanted to be what she saw him to be. A good guy. But he wasn't a good guy. Another reason why he couldn't touch her. He was no good for her, and she'd made her choice—Emilio. *He* was the good guy. Gone too soon. Leaving her a widow at twenty-nine. Leaving Alejandro without his friend.

With that last thought, his eyes lowered as sleep came over him.

～

THE FAINT CREAK of a door hinge broke the stillness of the night.

Alejandro's eyes opened, and as they adjusted to the darkness, he listened, his brow furrowed in concentration. He heard the faintest sound of movement and then the *snick* of the door leading to the carport closed.

Someone was in the house.

Not one person. More than one. Two.

One of them crept past the sofa, his body casting a moving shadow across the room. Alejandro's heart pounded in his chest. Whoever they were, he'd be able to take them by surprise.

He stood and saw a big man dressed in black near the door, and a shorter man—also in black—heading down the hall.

The shorter man must have sensed Alejandro's presence because he suddenly swung toward him and lifted a gun with a silencer on the tip. A second before he fired, Alejandro flung himself to the floor, and the lamp across the room shattered into pieces.

What the hell?

Alejandro snatched the glass from the table, and when the man edged around the sofa, he tossed it at his head and leaped up. One foot landed on the sofa cushions, springboarding him into a flying leap onto the man.

They slammed into the wall, and he gripped the man's throat with one hand and encircled his wrist holding the gun with his other. He slammed his hand twice against the wall to force him to drop the weapon.

"Drop it!" he growled.

He heard the big one behind him move and jerked the arm of the shorter man in the direction of his friend. Alejandro covered his finger with his and squeezed the trigger. The big man fell to the floor with a loud grunt.

He and the shorter man continued to wrestle. He could see the man's piercing blue eyes in the darkness, and his rancid breath was hot against Alejandro's cheek as they grappled for control. They crashed into the counter, the edge hitting hard against Alejandro's side. But he ignored the pain and took that opportunity to knock his opponent's hand on the edge of the bar. This time, the weapon slid across the bar top and onto the floor.

He landed a vicious right hook, and the bones in the intruder's jaw cracked and gave way. Then he slammed the man's head against the edge of the counter. He cried out in pain and made a half-hearted attempt to swing at Alejandro who dodged the blow and grabbed a handful of his dark hair, then banged his head on the counter again.

The door down the hall opened, and Alejandro turned in that direction. Camila was barely visible through the cracked door.

"Stay inside and lock the door!" he barked.

She quickly shut herself inside.

He spotted a pen left on the counter and stretched for his fingers to grab it. With a quick twist of his wrist, he drove the pen into the side of the man's neck. There was a sickening pop, and warm, sticky blood oozed from the side of his neck onto Alejandro's hand. He collapsed to the floor, his body twitching as the life drained from him.

Alejandro faded left at movement from the corner of his eye. The big man was on his feet, and the silver blade in his hand was marred by a thread of blood. Son of a bitch had cut him.

He swung the knife again, missing Alejandro's head by mere inches. The big man charged but slipped on his friend's blood, and Alejandro took advantage of his imbalance to land a throat punch. The blow would take down a lesser man, but not this guy. He was either impervious to pain or high as hell.

The guy swung the knife, but Alejandro blocked the blow and followed up with a punch to the gut that didn't seem to faze the intruder at all. Back and forth they went, Alejandro keeping his distance, lighter on his feet than the man who was several inches taller and at least fifty pounds heavier.

He grabbed a pot from the counter and swung, knocking the knife from the man's hand. That infuriated the giant. He charged with a growl filled with anger and adrenaline. He seized Alejandro by the throat and hit his head against the wall. The world blurred as pain exploded inside his skull.

But he quickly retaliated with a knee to the gut. The impact forced a grunt from the intruder, but he didn't let go. They twisted and turned, like two ancient warriors fighting to the death. They bounced off the counter, banged into the sofa, and knocked knickknacks to the floor.

Punch. Block. Grapple. Twist. Gasp. Grunt. Neither willing to give in.

They wrestled their way down the hall, stumbling into the

wall and knocking a photo to the floor. The bastard was strong, and Alejandro's muscles burned with the effort of fighting him.

He shoved Alejandro through the half-open bathroom door, and they crashed into the small space, the sound of their grunts echoing off the walls. He swung, and Alejandro ducked, sliding behind him to grab him in a full Nelson—arms under his arms, hands locked behind his neck. He stood on his toes and applied pressure to force a compression choke.

Arms flailing, the man fought for air. He twisted and turned, but Alejandro tightened the hold, his fingers in an unbreakable S lock. He thought for a moment he had him good, but the giant had a burst of energy and flung himself backward.

Alejandro lost his balance, and they crashed into one end of the tub. His back hit the tiled wall and pain shot through his shoulders. The curtain yanked the rings and they snapped, clattering into the tub with the rod.

Thinking fast, Alejandro wrapped the plastic curtain around the man's head and used his strong legs to force his arms flat against his body. The intruder thrashed wildly and roared like an angry bear, but Alejandro wouldn't let go. Muffled screams filled the bathroom, and Alejandro's muscles burned as he tightened his grip on the body jerking between his thighs.

The struggle seemed to last for an eternity. The giant continued to fight, his movements violent as he fought for breath, forcing Alejandro to grit his teeth and hold on tight. He held firm to the shower curtain and kept his legs locked around the man's arms. Muscles tight, his fingers strained with the effort, and his knuckles turned white as he used every last bit of strength he had left.

Finally, the giant's movements slowed and then stopped altogether. In the ensuing silence, only Alejandro's ragged breathing could be heard. Chest heaving, he rested his head against the tile and momentarily closed his eyes.

He took one deep, calming breath and then shoved the life-less body off him. The smell of sweat, blood, and fear lingered in the air, a reminder of the brutal fight for survival that had taken place.

Alejandro pushed to his feet and turned on the light. He stared at the dead man—his black T-shirt soaked with blood from the round that had torn through him. Incredible. He had fought as if he hadn't been shot.

He stepped out of the bathroom and listened to the quiet of the house, making sure no one else had entered. All threats had been eliminated.

Satisfied, he flicked on the hall light and went to knock on Camila's bedroom door.

7

When Alejandro called out to Camila, she was hiding in the corner beside her bed, gripping a collapsible baton that Alejandro had advised her to purchase years ago because she went on early morning walks to plan the day. He was always concerned about her safety and regularly gave her advice, reminding her to pay attention to her surroundings and trust her instincts.

She had called the police and hurriedly pulled jeans and a blouse over her nightclothes but otherwise didn't know what to do as she listened to the struggle outside—horror and dread fighting for supremacy in every beat of her heart. She had wanted to help but had been afraid to open the door—not to mention Alejandro would be furious if she did.

She opened the door now, and what she saw made her drop the baton and gape at her friend. "Is that your blood?" she whispered.

Red smears streaked his hands, his tattooed arms, his torso, the tribal tattoo on his left pec, as well as his rumpled gray shorts. Despite his appearance and their current situation, she couldn't help but admire his physique. Every muscle was defined, like someone whose full-time job was working out.

He glanced down at his body, as if he hadn't noticed the blood. "I got a nick on my right arm. The rest belongs to the intruders."

How could he speak so calmly after what had occurred?

"Where are they?" She tried to see past him.

"I took care of them."

"What does that mean?" she asked.

"They're dead. Both of them. One in the kitchen and one in the bathroom."

Camila didn't know what to say. She'd heard him fighting and yet, knowing they'd died was a shock. She knew Alejandro could handle himself. He was a bodyguard, after all, and when they were younger he had always been big, tough, and had a mean streak. Yet knowing he had killed those men left her speechless.

"Do you think they came here to kill me? What if you hadn't been here?" She was talking too fast and sounded panicked.

"Don't worry about what could have happened. I was here, and that is all that matters."

She pressed a hand to her forehead. "Nothing like this has ever happened to me, Alejandro. I-I don't understand why they broke into my home."

"We're going to find out—why they're here and who they are. Did you call the police?"

She nodded.

"Okay. Do you have disposable gloves or cleaning gloves?"

"I-I..." She was having a hard time thinking. "I have disposable ones under the sink in the bathroom."

"Good. This is what I want you to do." His commanding tone made her pay attention. "Go into the car and lock the doors. Drive a couple of blocks down the street and keep the engine running. If you see anything out of the ordinary—anything at all—I want you to leave."

"Leave you?"

"Yes."

She didn't like his answer. She'd suffered so much loss in the past three years, what if she lost him too? She could have tonight.

"I will be fine," he said, looking directly into her eyes. "But I want to make sure you stay safe. It's possible more men could be on their way here, and I want to make sure that if there is any more danger, you can escape. Understood?"

"Yes, but—"

"We will talk later. For now, I want you to do as I tell you."

"Okay."

"Go."

Shaking, Camila grabbed her purse and keys and walked through the house with Alejandro close behind her. She glanced briefly at the dead man on the floor. Something was sticking out of his neck, but she quickly averted her gaze from the sickening sight.

As Alejandro watched, she started the car and backed out of the carport. Though the danger had passed her heart was racing. She didn't understand what had happened—how they had gone from celebrating with family and friends to a bloody crime scene.

She drove the car down the street and shoved it in park. She kept the engine running as he had instructed. Eyes darting around the neighborhood, she sat there, waiting for the police to arrive.

∼

ALEJANDRO MOVED QUICKLY, going into his bedroom and removing his phone from the nightstand. He wouldn't have

much time before the police showed up. He hadn't changed
clothes because he wanted the crime scene investigators to
collect as much DNA off him and his shorts as they could.

He went into the bathroom and found the gloves under the
sink. They were a tight fit for his hands but would work for
what he had planned.

He started with the man in the bathroom. Shifting him
sideways, he removed his wallet from his back pocket and
searched through the contents. Using his own phone, he
snapped a photo of the man's driver's license. There was
nothing else in the wallet of interest, but with a quick pat down
he found a set of keys, which he took.

Next, he searched the man he'd laid out near the kitchen.
He didn't have a wallet on him but had cigarettes, a lighter, and
keys. Alejandro took the keys and rushed outside.

Camila was parked down the street. Good.

Walking around outside, he pressed the key fobs of both
sets of keys. Finally, he heard a car squawk on the next block.
He raced between the houses and saw the car, its lights
blinking on and off. He entered the vehicle right as he heard
the sound of police sirens. *Mierda*. They didn't sound too far
away. He'd have to hurry.

He searched the car, taking photos of papers he found in
the glove compartment, indicating the car belonged to the big
guy. He found an impressive stash of weapons in the trunk but
nothing else of interest. He locked the car, raced back to the
house, and returned the keys to the pocket of each man. He
tossed the gloves and then went down the street to where
Camila was parked.

He tapped the driver's window. "I'm going to stay out here. I
don't want to contaminate your car."

"Okay. What did you find?" she asked anxiously.

"A bunch of weapons in their car. I took a photo of one of

the men's I.D. I have his name and address. Richard Larson. Ring a bell?"

Camila shook her head.

Alejandro's eyes flicked to the approaching squad cars with flashing lights. "When the police are gone, we can discuss why someone was sent to your house to kill you. Because that's why they were here. They had weapons. One a knife, the other a gun. Their weapons were already out when they entered the house."

Her eyes widened.

"We also need to figure out who sent them," Alejandro added.

That was the most confusing part. Camila wasn't tangled up in anything illicit, and he doubted she had enemies. So why would someone want to kill her?

They stopped talking when the three police cars pulled up and blocked the street. Alejandro caught a neighbor peeking through a window before pulling the curtain closed again.

Camila exited the vehicle to stand beside him as a female officer approached.

"Ms. Hughes?"

"Yes." Camila stepped forward.

"I'm Officer Jenkins." She looked at Alejandro. "And you are?"

"Alejandro Sanchez, a friend."

"Sir, are you hurt?" Her eyes swept his body with concern.

"No. The blood isn't mine."

"Whose is it?"

"The men who broke into my home. They're both inside— dead," Camila replied.

The officer appeared startled by what she said. "All right. We're going to secure the scene. Other than the intruders, is there anyone else in the house?"

"No."

"Do you have any weapons on your person?"

"No."

A male officer stepped forward to frisk Alejandro while Officer Jenkins patted down Camila.

When they finished, Officer Jenkins seemed satisfied. "Please stay here." She walked toward the house with the other officers following her.

Alejandro and Camila turned to each other. They didn't have to say a word. They both knew it was going to be a long night.

8

After CSI had taken photos of Alejandro and DNA from his body, he changed clothes. He donned jeans and a dark shirt with the sleeves cut off. Then an EMT sat him in the back of the ambulance and tended to the cut on his right arm. It had been bleeding, but luckily the slice wasn't deep.

Camila stood nearby, arms folded as she watched the police activity around her home. Crime scene tape blocked off the area, and the flashing lights of the police vehicles swept across the houses and had awakened several of her neighbors who watched the activity from their front doors.

"Okay, you're all set," the female EMT said, giving Alejandro a toothy grin.

"Thank you," he said, getting to his feet with a bandage on his arm. He walked over to Camila.

"I'm sure she would love to do more than fix your cut," Camila muttered.

"You think everyone wants to sleep with me."

Because they do, she thought.

A black Buick sedan rolled up to the scene, and Camila groaned when she saw the detective step out.

"You know him?" Alejandro asked.

"Yes. That's Detective Slater, and he's an ass."

His skin was light brown and so were his eyes. He approached wearing a dark suit and a lazy swagger. "Well, if it isn't our favorite Blaxican reporter. Looks like tonight you're the news instead of writing about it."

"Nice to see you, Detective," she said in a dry tone.

"We both know you don't mean that. Who's this?"

"Alejandro Sanchez," Alejandro replied.

"I'm Detective Slater."

Both men shook hands.

"Alejandro is a friend from out of town. He saved my life tonight."

"A friend, huh?" Detective Slater looked up at Alejandro's imposing height and then let his gaze drop to his tatted arms.

Camila stiffened. She didn't like what he was implying but kept her mouth shut since her relationship with Alejandro was none of his business.

"Give me a few minutes to talk to the officers, and then I'll be back to interview the two of you."

While they waited for him to return, several more neighbors came out of their homes to gawk at the scene. Fifteen minutes later, the detective returned.

"Okay, as I understand it, there were two intruders. What happened?" He removed a small notebook from his inside jacket pocket.

"They broke into my home. One had a gun, and one had a knife," Camila answered.

"I saw, but they're both dead."

"Thanks to Alejandro."

The detective silently observed Alejandro, who looked right back at him.

"Care to explain how you did that?"

"We fought, and I got lucky."

He eyed Alejandro with suspicion. "Uh-huh. Walk me through what happened."

Listening to her friend recount the story was terrifying, not only for herself, as she understood he was the only reason she was alive and breathing. But she fully appreciated he could have been killed.

Detective Slater took information from them both. At the end of the interview, he flipped back to the start of his notebook. "Let me run through this one more time. You came home and were asleep when these men entered the house and attacked. You have no idea who they are or why they're here." He lifted his gaze to Camila.

"Correct. We were gone all night and said goodbye to my brother and the other wedding guests sometime after two. We were completely taken by surprise."

The detective tapped his pen on the notepad. "Forensics is going over their car in detail, and of course you know you can't stay here tonight. Do you have someplace where you can stay?"

"Well, my par—"

"We'll get a hotel," Alejandro interrupted her.

She looked at him. "Right," she agreed.

"Good idea. Mr. Sanchez, I'm very impressed that you were able to take down both men by yourself. Who are you, exactly?"

"What do you mean?"

"I assume you have a military background."

"I'm not military. I work for a company called The Cordoba Agency. You're welcome to look them up, if you like. We provide security and investigative services for clients."

"Bodyguards?"

"Yes, among other services."

The detective peered directly into his eyes. Challenging him. "A lot of you guys have military backgrounds, don't you?"

"Not me."

"If not a military background, maybe a criminal background? Maybe these men were here for you and not Ms. Hughes."

"What's the point of this, Detective Slater?" Camila demanded. "He *saved* my life. If he hadn't been here, I would be dead."

Detective Slater shrugged. "Just doing my job, that's all."

"I assure you, Alejandro has nothing to do with what happened here tonight. We're the victims. You need to look into these men. Maybe this isn't the first home invasion they've done."

"No need to get snippy," Detective Slater said irritably. "I'm trying to do my damn job. I have to ask these questions, as I'm sure you know."

Alejandro took a step forward to stand beside Camila instead of right behind her. "Maybe you should watch your tone. Are we done here?" He spoke in a calm voice, but anyone with functioning ears could detect the cold undertones.

Detective Slater smirked. "Yes, we're done. Have a good night, Mr. Sanchez. You too, Camila." He turned away and then swung back around. "How long will you be here, Mr. Sanchez?"

"For as long as it takes," Alejandro answered.

The detective narrowed his eyes. "For as long as what takes?"

"For as long as it takes for you to find out why Camila's home was broken into."

"We might never find out."

"Then I'll never leave."

Both men stared at each other, then the detective flashed a smile. "Wouldn't want to keep you here unnecessarily. I'm sure you want to get home as quickly as possible. I'll be sure to work extra hard to make sure we solve this case so you can." He walked away, ducking under the tape to go talk to one of the uniformed officers.

Alejandro glared at his retreating back.

"You don't like him," Camila said.

"No, and the feeling is mutual. Let's pack a bag and get out of here. I didn't want to mention where we were going to the detective. He gives me a bad vibe. For now, we don't trust anyone."

"We can stay at my parents' place. It's empty."

"Are you sure?"

"I can handle it. Being there isn't the problem. It's letting go that's hard."

His gaze was sympathetic. "All right. We'll stay there."

With an officer's permission, they packed their bags and left the house. They both remained silent, deep in their own thoughts as Alejandro drove them to her parents' two-story house and parked the car in the garage.

Camila took the master bedroom, and Alejandro took the guest room down the hall. After they deposited their belongings in the rooms, they reconvened in the living room downstairs. He sat in one of the armchairs, and she sat cross-legged on the sofa.

"Is it possible you wrote an article that pissed someone off?" Alejandro asked.

"Me?" Camila laughed. "Most of my pieces are about the nightlife or activities to do in town. You know that. They're puff pieces or human-interest stories. I rarely write anything hard-hitting."

"You don't think it's possible you wrote something that could have upset someone?"

"It's possible," Camila said slowly, rubbing her forehead, "but unlikely. I'd have to think about it. Certainly nothing recently." She sighed wearily. "I don't know. I'm at the point where I'm too tired to think."

"You should get some rest."

"What about you?"

"Can't sleep. I'm wired."

"Are you okay? Other than the cut on your arm, I don't think you have a scratch on you from those guys."

"Some bruising, but no more cuts," Alejandro said with a cocky grin.

"Same old Jandro," she teased, unfolding her legs.

"What time are we meeting your brother and his friends for lunch?"

"Twelve-thirty." Her brother and his new bride were flying to Mexico later that afternoon. The rest of his friends were going to finish the weekend in Vegas and fly out the following day.

"We have the name and address of one of the men. I'll go by his apartment and see if I can find any information."

"I'm coming with you," Camila said.

"No," Alejandro said with finality.

"Yes, I am."

"Camila—"

"Alejandro, I'm coming with you. If you want me to stay in the car, I'll do that, but I want to know who these men are just as much as you do."

He was silent as he looked at her, and she refused to show weakness by dropping her gaze first.

"We'll do that, for now, but at the first sign of danger, you're staying your butt out of the way."

"Fine. Not a problem."

"One more thing, we'll need to rent a car. Something less conspicuous than that purple monstrosity."

"Was that really necessary?" Camila asked, watching him as he rose from the chair.

"I'm going to take a shower," he announced, heading toward the stairs.

She watched him leave and then sat quietly, thinking about the night. How had Alejandro been able to do what he did? She had made jokes in the past about him being in the FBI but knew he had worked for the U.S. government at one point, though he had been very secretive about it.

In fact, that's how they'd lost touch at one time. After he had been thrown into prison. She had been worried sick. Only seventeen, and what he'd done—while illegal—had been noble. Then he was gone, and she never saw or heard from him for more than two years.

She had missed him, but she had never worried. Somehow she knew he would turn up again. Emilio had been sweet and kind. She had always worried about Emilio, but never about Alejandro.

The next time she saw him, he was different. Almost twenty. More mature. More muscular. He had become a man with a dangerous edge who observed the world around him with quiet intensity. He was like a wolf—no, bigger and more dangerous— a tiger.

From then on, he would disappear for months at a time. "Top-secret government work," he always said, but nothing more. For the longest time, she couldn't tell if he was kidding or not.

Whatever his training, they had turned him into a killing machine, for which she was thankful. He'd saved her life tonight.

Camila rose from the sofa and turned out the light. She climbed the stairs, and as she passed the hall bathroom on the way to her parents' old room, she heard the shower running.

She stopped inches past the doorframe and strained her ears to listen. Her mind flashed back to his appearance outside her bedroom. Despite having blood and sweat all over him, he looked like sex poured into long legs and swarthy skin.

Now she imagined all that dark, muscular flesh being

covered in water and soap as he cleaned his body. What she wouldn't give to be a soap bubble right now.

The shower stopped, shaking her from her reverie. She scurried to the bedroom—running from being discovered and running from the thoughts that threatened to consume her.

9

The following morning, Alejandro and Camila sat across the street from Richard Larson's apartment complex—the big man who had broken into her house. They had left her car in her parents' garage, and Alejandro had rented a gray Honda Accord from a small lot. Much less conspicuous.

Initially, he planned to break into Larson's bottom unit and search the place, but when they rode past, there was a blue pickup truck parked outside and the front door was ajar. They drove past the complex and went across the street to park in front of an insurance office that didn't open until ten.

While they watched, a burly redhead took items from the apartment and placed them in the truck. He had a full beard, no mustache, and a belly that made him look seven months pregnant.

"Do you think he's a thief?" Camila asked quietly.

Alejandro shook his head. "He is moving too confidently for a thief. He's supposed to be there."

"If he's supposed to be there, he must have made plans with Richard before, or he knows Richard is dead."

"I believe it's the second, which means someone tipped him off. But why is he taking his things? It's mostly electronics."

"I didn't notice, but you're right. The Samsung TVs, the computer."

Finally, the redhead locked the apartment. He gave his surroundings a cursory review and then climbed into the truck. Alejandro started the car and followed at a safe distance, keeping two cars between them most of the time. They didn't have to follow him for long. After ten minutes, he pulled into the parking lot of Luxury Pawn.

Alejandro drove past the spot and parked on the side of the building.

"I'll wait a few minutes until he has taken everything inside, and then I'll go in and ask him a few questions."

"I'm coming with you."

He sighed heavily, like a parent dealing with an obstinate child. "No, you're not."

"Why not?" Camila demanded in an exasperated voice.

"Because we do not know who this man is, and you need to be careful."

"I'm not a delicate little flower, Alejandro. I can take care of myself. Besides, what can possibly happen if I'm with you?"

"I appreciate your confidence, but—"

"But nothing. I'm coming, and you can't stop me. If he knows anything about the men who broke into my house, I want to know what he knows."

Alejandro shook his head in annoyance.

"Don't give me that look. Besides, I might be able to help you."

"You will get in the way."

"We'll see about that."

He shot her another look. "If you're going to come with me, you need to listen to me and follow my lead."

"I can do that," she promised.

He hesitated, but then said, "Okay, this is what I'm going to do..." He spent the next few minutes explaining his plan.

After a short wait, they climbed out of the car and walked into the pawn shop, Camila ahead of Alejandro—her tight jeans hugging her hips, ponytail swinging as her head turned on a swivel. A small bell above the door tinkled when they entered. Alejandro's gaze swept the interior, noting shelves filled with all types of merchandise—radios, TVs, tablets, and binoculars. As they approached the counter, he also noted that the light on the wall camera was off, indicating it didn't work.

"Hello, welcome to Luxury Pawn. How can I help you?" the redhead asked in a jovial voice.

"*Hola amigo*, I'm looking for a television. I have a preference for Samsung. Do you have one?" Alejandro asked.

Camila walked over to a wall where the shelves were filled with small kitchen appliances.

"Samsung, huh? I have a forty-inch over there." He pointed toward the back of the store, where there were several televisions.

"I was looking for something a little larger. Say... a forty-eight inch?" Alejandro asked.

"Forty-eight inches, huh?" The guy stroked his beard. "Well, it so happens I just got something in, and it's practically brand new. I haven't had a chance to put a price on it yet."

"Oh really? Can I see it? The wife and I have been looking for something affordable that works in our son's room." Alejandro flashed a smile at the guy, but talking about their imaginary son made his insides twist.

"Well... okay. Hang on." The man disappeared in the back, and Camila walked up to the counter.

"He's going to bring the one we saw him take from the apartment," she whispered.

"Shh," Alejandro said out the corner of his mouth.

The man brought out the television and placed it on the counter. "Here she is."

"That's nice. How much?" Camila asked.

"Give me two fifty cash, and it's yours."

"One fifty," Camila said.

The man laughed. "Too low. How about two-twenty-five? A television like this is worth at least a thousand dollars if bought brand new, and this one works like a charm. I'll even throw in the remote so you don't have to buy one."

"Two hundred," Alejandro interjected.

He shook his head regretfully. "I need to make my money back. Remember, I had to buy this from a customer, and the margins are really small."

"Which customer did you buy this from?" Camila asked.

Oh shit.

The man's smile faltered. "Huh?"

Camila repeated the question. "Which customer did you buy the television from?"

"What she means is—"

"That's none of your business." The owner looked at both of them with the beginnings of suspicion.

"We know you picked up this television and some other items from Larson's apartment. What we want to know is, who told you to pick up the items?" Camila demanded.

"What's it to you? Are you cops?" the man asked.

"He's a friend of mine," Camila said.

"Bull. Shit."

Camila rested her hands on her hips. "We saw you taking the items out of the apartment, and we're pretty sure he didn't give you permission to take his things and pawn them."

"You don't know shit. Get the fuck out of my shop." The man's face turned apple-red.

"No need to get upset," Alejandro interjected in a calming

tone. The conversation was going downhill and the guy was looking rather twitchy.

"Oh yeah? The two of you came in here and basically accused me of stealing. I don't appreciate that."

"If you didn't steal it, then it's not a problem, right?" Camila said. "Tell us who told you to get the items, and we'll be on our way."

The man reached under the counter and pulled out a Beretta. Camila gasped, and Alejandro yanked her behind him, fixing a friendly smile on his face and lifting his hands in a disarming way.

"Listen, *güey*, we don't want any trouble."

"Then get out of my shop with your accusations. I don't know nothing about no Richard Larson. Whatever you're trying to pin on me, I ain't having it."

"Fair enough. We made a mistake. We'll leave you alone now." Alejandro took a step back and bumped into Camila. "Let's go, *honey*," he said through gritted teeth.

Whenever a gun was pointed at him in a situation like this, it was better to keep the perpetrator and the weapon in his eyesight, so he continued backing up.

When Camila opened the door, the owner yelled, "And don't come back in here, or I'm calling the cops!"

They exited the building and went to the car. Camila climbed into the passenger seat. Clutching her chest, she took several deep breaths. "Oh, my goodness. That didn't go well."

"I told you not to come."

"Gee, thanks."

"I told you to follow my lead. I know what I'm doing."

"I'm sorry! The conversation was going so slow, and I wanted answers!"

Resting his arm on her seat, Alejandro leaned in. "And how did the conversation progress when you took the lead? Did you get the information you wanted?"

She opened her mouth and closed it again.

"This isn't one of your magazine interviews. We're dealing with dangerous people, as you saw."

She slumped in the seat, looking defeated. "Now what?"

Alejandro felt bad as he watched her crestfallen expression. He softened his voice. "It was possible he didn't know whose apartment he had raided, but now we know he did know. We never told him Richard's full name. You said Larson. He said Richard Larson."

She blinked. "You're right, but how does that help us?"

"It doesn't." Alejandro climbed out of the car.

"Where are you going?" Camila asked.

He shut the door and headed toward the pawn shop, answering over his shoulder, "I forgot something."

She opened her door. "What did you forget?"

Instead of answering, Alejandro took long-legged strides back to the shop and re-entered. The bell above the door jingled again, and the owner came out from the back.

When he saw Alejandro coming at him, he tensed. "The fuck, man. I told you I don't know nothing. Get the fuck out of my shop."

Alejandro kept walking toward him, and the redhead finally figured out the situation was going downhill. His eyes widened, and he reached under the counter again, but Alejandro was ready this time. He rushed forward with a long stride, grabbed the back of the man's head, and slammed his face into the wooden surface. He let out a squeal of pain as blood burst from his nose.

Alejandro yanked him over the counter, knocking papers and products to the floor. The redhead fell to the floor with a groan, and Alejandro grabbed him by the collar and forced him to his feet.

"Wait, stop—"

Alejandro shoved him against a load-bearing wall. Pressing

an arm across his throat, he leaned in close enough to see the different shades of red in his beard.

"The woman outside saved you earlier. I don't like for her to see my violent side. She's not in here now, which means I don't give a fuck. So, you're going to answer my questions right now, ¿*comprendes*?"

"Yeah, yeah, *comprendes*," he replied in a quivering voice that strained from the pressure Alejandro applied.

Alejandro didn't bother correcting his Spanish. "Who told you to go pick up those items from Larson's house? No bullshit this time. We saw you take the items from his apartment."

The man frowned, then he burst out laughing.

"What is so funny, *pendejo*?" Alejandro yanked him forward and shoved him against the wall again.

The man winced and swallowed hard. "You think I'm going to tell you anything."

"You are a lot dumber than you look."

"I'm not talking, man. No way, no how. They'll kill me, man."

"Who?"

He clamped his mouth shut.

"Listen to me. You need to be worried about me—the man standing in front of you—and no one else. Death will be a blessing compared to what I'll do to you if I close this shop early and take you in the back room."

The man gulped and fear filled his eyes.

"Who told you to go to his apartment and get his things?"

"You gotta promise me you won't repeat where you got this information from. I have a family, man."

"And yet you're mixed up with people who could kill you if you talk?"

He shrugged. "Gotta do what I gotta do."

Alejandro paused and stared into his eyes. "How do I know you'll tell me the truth?"

"You'll know. I wouldn't make this up."

"Okay, you have my word."

He took a deep breath and closed his eyes. Slowly, he opened them again. "I received a call from Javier Reyes's assistant. If you don't know who he is, he owns the Celestial Palace. His assistant told me there had been an incident and Larson was dead. Said if I wanted the stuff, it was mine, but I should go in there and get it now before the cops showed up."

"Why would he call you?"

"He and I go way back. We've helped each other out over the years."

"Helped how?" Alejandro asked.

"If he needs weapons or whatever—I'm his guy. In exchange, he lets me know about opportunities like this. He's worked for Reyes for years."

Alejandro eased up on his throat. "What does Reyes have to do with this?"

He chuckled. "You don't know, huh? Larson was one of Reyes's guys. A fixer. He got rid of problems, but apparently someone took care of him this time."

"And the assistant found out because he works for Reyes."

"Exactly." The man wiped away the blood dripping from his nose.

"You have been very helpful."

"You'll keep your end of the bargain?"

"I will. And make sure you don't pass on any information to your friend. If you betray me, I know where to find you." He dropped his arm and stepped back.

"Believe me, I won't say a word. I don't want anybody to know I had anything to do with you. You better be careful if you're messing with the Reyes family, man. Alvaro Reyes was a thug, but his son, Javier? The guy's a fucking lunatic."

Alejandro digested that bit of information. "Good to know."

He walked out of the store, the little bell above the door tinkling as he left.

He climbed behind the wheel, and Camila looked at him expectantly.

"What did you do?"

"I asked the questions again. Nicely, this time."

"Nicely? Why do I doubt that?"

Alejandro started the car and glanced at her. "You're not going to believe what I found out."

10

Camila and Alejandro met Miguel and the rest of the wedding guests for a goodbye lunch at twelve-thirty as planned, but she could barely concentrate on eating after what Alejandro had told her. She remembered the look Javier Reyes had sent in her direction the night before and the unease she'd felt. Had he really dispatched someone to her house to kill her, and if so—why?

She didn't tell her brother about the break-in because she didn't want him to worry. He should have an enjoyable visit to Mexico to see family first before he and his new wife took off for a worry-free honeymoon in Hawaii, and Alejandro agreed.

When lunch ended, they all said goodbye. She hugged her brother and her new sister-in-law and wished them a safe trip.

After she and Alejandro separated from the rest of the group, a wave of sadness overcame her. Miguel was moving on with his life, and she seemed to be at a standstill. Soon he would begin his career as a biotechnologist and then start a family. She would still be in Las Vegas, unsure if she wanted to stay there but unable to make a decision about where she wanted to go next.

As Alejandro drove toward her parents' house, a local news update caught her attention, and she turned up the volume on the radio. The DJ had been giving the afternoon update on the weather and traffic, but a female reporter had broken in with a hot story.

"...the body was found behind the Abner's Market building. The victim appears to be a local homeless man. We don't know much at the moment, except he was shot, and police are on the scene now."

The DJ returned, his upbeat voice in stark contrast to the solemnity of the reporter who had given the devastating news.

Camila turned off the radio and glanced at Alejandro. She couldn't breathe. "I have to go down there. I have to know if it's Doug."

"Let's go," he said in a grim tone, as if he had been thinking the same thing and already knew what they'd find.

She didn't want *anyone* to be dead, but she hoped the dead man wasn't Doug. She would be devastated.

She gave Alejandro directions, but the drive to Abner's Market seemed to take forever. When they arrived on the scene, police officers were everywhere, and the area behind the small grocery store was cordoned off with police tape. She saw Detective Slater right away. His rumpled suit suggested he had worked all night without going home.

Camila walked up to the police tape. "Hi, Detective Slater."

He lifted an eyebrow when he saw them. "Well, well, well, if it isn't our favorite Blaxican reporter again. This isn't the type of story you usually report on in *The Pulse*."

Camila refrained from rolling her eyes and played nice. "I know, but I'm curious about the victim."

"Why? You think he might be one of yours?"

Her series of articles about the homeless had been popular. "Invisible Lives: Stories from the Streets" had resulted in her becoming a minor celebrity when local news channels invited her on their shows for interviews.

"Possibly," Camila replied, a knot forming in her stomach. "Have you ID'd the victim?"

He sent a curious look in Alejandro's direction. "I see you have your bodyguard with you."

Alejandro stood a little ways back, feet braced apart and thumbs hooked in the belt loop of his jeans. His expression was emotionless as he looked right back at the detective with barely concealed contempt.

"He told you he'd be here for a while," Camila reminded him.

Detective Slater muttered something under his breath and pulled out his notepad. "The body is of a male. Caucasian. About five-ten, looks like he's in his fifties, but those guys usually look older than they really are. Nothing special about him, really."

Camila stopped breathing. "Does he have a birthmark on the inside of his right arm—sort of resembles a boot?"

The detective flipped up a page on his little notebook. "Yeah."

Camila's heart tanked.

Seeing the look on her face, he asked, "That your guy?"

Camila nodded, unable to speak around the lump in her throat.

His forehead puckered. "You got a name for him?"

"Doug. Doug Duvall," Camila answered in a soft voice.

He wrote down the name. He was unconcerned and clinical in his questioning while she was falling apart inside.

"How long has he been back there?" Camila asked.

"Best guess right now is a few days, but we should have a better idea once the ME gets him on the table for a thorough examination."

"I heard on the radio that he was shot?"

"Yeah." He pursed his lips and shook his head. "Looks like he gave up."

His comment startled her. "Gave up? What do you mean?"

"No final word yet, but the ME said his death looks like suicide. Gun by his side, a bullet to the temple." He positioned his hand to the right of his head and acted like he pulled the trigger.

The crude gesture shocked her, but his answer was even more shocking. "No way. Impossible."

"Why is that impossible?"

"Doug couldn't have killed himself, Detective. I found his sister for him."

"Sweetheart, you know how these people are. You wrote a whole series about them. They're hooked on drugs and alcohol because they're running from their pasts or whatever demons are chasing them. Hell, they disappear all the time without a trace. Did he know you'd found his sister?"

"*Yes!* She's coming to pick him up tomorrow. Their reunion has been planned for weeks."

His left eyebrow arched in surprise. "All right, calm down. You have the sister's information?"

Camila took a calming breath. She shouldn't let him get her so riled up, but his indifference was typical and infuriating. "Her name is Melissa Duvall." Camila pulled out her phone and gave him Melissa's phone number.

"Got it." He tapped his pen on the notepad. "Look, I know you don't want to hear this, but it's clear the poor bastard gave up before she could arrive. Maybe he couldn't handle seeing her or didn't want her to see him in his current condition."

"I don't believe that," Camila said in a firm voice.

"The facts speak for themselves." He shrugged.

"Could you wait before you call his sister? I'd like to tell her myself what happened."

"Sure. I've got plenty to do otherwise. I'll give her a ring first thing in the morning." He gave her shoulder an awkward pat in a condescending way. "Can't save them all, sweetheart."

He walked away, leaving her to stare after him.

Asshole.

She walked over to Alejandro. "Did you hear what he said?" He nodded.

"I don't understand why Doug would do that. It doesn't make sense. *Kill himself?*" She lifted her eyes, seeking the answers from him.

"It happens. There are lots of people who seem fine on the outside and are suffering on the inside. Friends and family only find out about their suffering when they take their own life."

"That's true, but..." Camila shook her head vehemently. "Not Doug. He had too much to live for."

"You're looking at the situation from your perspective. Like the detective said, he could have had his own demons that you don't know about."

"I'm not convinced, Alejandro," she said.

His gaze traveled over the busy scene of police and crime scene techs. "You are confident he would not have killed himself?" he asked.

"He didn't have a death wish. Not the Doug that I knew. Plus, like I said, I'd found his sister, and his dog Poodle is with Rhonda at the homeless encampment downtown. He wouldn't have left Poodle alone without making some kind of arrangement. She was his baby."

"How sure are you?" Alejandro asked.

She paused. He was right, lots of people held their hurt inside and believed the only way to have relief was to end their life. But not this time. Not Doug. "A thousand percent sure, and I plan to do something about it."

A wary expression crossed his features. "Camila..."

She dropped her voice. "I'm going to do a little investigating myself. Couldn't hurt."

"Someone tried to kill you!" Alejandro reminded her in a fierce whisper. "We haven't figured that out yet."

"It could have been a simple burglary."

"By one of Reyes's men?" he reminded her.

Right. She had forgotten about that.

"I don't know why Reyes sent men after me, but what I do know is the cops are not going to dig into Doug's death, which was the message of the series I wrote. People like Doug are invisible to society at large, and Detective Slater said the ME already suspects it's a suicide. They're not going to launch a full investigation when they can simply call him a drunk homeless man and say he killed himself. I'm not going to let them sweep his death under the rug and close out the case because he doesn't fit society's idea of a person of value. Doug deserved better and his sister deserves better. Real answers. I don't think it was suicide, and I intend to find out who killed him."

Muttering a few choice curse words under his breath, Alejandro studied her for a moment as she anxiously waited for his reply.

"If you're going to look into his death, you will need help. Since I'm staying anyway, I'll help you."

"You were serious about staying? Don't you have to go back to work?"

"I have some flexibility in my schedule."

"Are you sure it won't be a problem?" Camila asked, though grateful.

"I am not leaving until I know you're safe." Alejandro started walking to the car.

Camila fell into step beside him. "You can't put your life on hold for me."

"I can do whatever the hell I want, and there's no way I'm letting you look into Doug's death by yourself. I don't like any of this. There is a lot happening in a short period of time, and I don't think it's a coincidence."

"You think the break-in at my house and Doug's death are connected?" She couldn't see how.

"Possibly. The only way to know for sure is to keep digging."

11

Back at the house, Alejandro sat on the sofa, phone to his ear, while Camila dialed the number for Doug's sister. This was going to be a tough conversation, and she understood how Doug's sister was about to feel because she'd had similar painful conversations in recent years.

Almost four years ago she found out her husband had been in a fatal accident. The following year she received the call that her father had died from complications with leukemia. A couple of years later, her mother passed away from heart failure. She took hit after hit, each call changing her life forever. She'd been hurt, disillusioned, and numb for weeks. Now she would be the one relaying information that would destroy another person.

She could imagine the disappointment and devastation Melissa would experience—finding her brother after all these years—only to lose him before they could meet.

At Melissa's cheery greeting, Camila almost wished she hadn't picked up the phone so she'd have more time to think of what to say, but she couldn't delay. Detective Slater would be calling in the morning.

"Hi, Melissa," Camila said, much more subdued.

"Hey there! What's up? If you've called to tell me my brother has changed his mind, tell him that he can't weasel out of our reunion. I've told the whole family, and we're planning a big welcome home party for him." She laughed, as if she'd told the best joke, certain there was no way Doug would cancel when he was about to be reunited with his family.

"Melissa, I need you to sit down. I have some bad news," Camila said, her voice quivering. She folded her feet under her in the armchair, her eyes resting on Alejandro as he spoke quietly to his boss to let him know he would remain in Vegas for longer than expected.

"Wait a minute, I was kidding. He hasn't changed his mind about moving in with me, has he? Is that why he hasn't returned my calls?"

"No, that's not why," Camila said gently. "Melissa, I don't know any other way to say this, but... Doug passed away. The police found his body."

Silence filled the line, and Camila hesitated to break it by speaking.

"Are you sure? Did *you* see his body?" Melissa asked in a strained voice.

"No, but the detective on the scene confirmed the birthmark on his arm."

"No." Her voice cracked on the word. "I don't understand. What happened?"

Hearing Melissa's pain caused grief to tighten her throat. "He was shot, and the police think it was self-inflicted," Camila replied in a low voice.

"They think he *killed* himself? That doesn't make any sense. How would he get a gun?"

"It doesn't make sense to me, either. The medical examiner has the final word, but that's what was suggested when I was at the scene."

"No. No. I don't believe he would kill himself. We just found each other again. I was coming to pick him up. I'll be there tomorrow. We talked about this. We talked about this. *We talked about this*, Camila."

Her voice ended on a heartrending wail. Then she quietly sobbed into the phone. Camila remained quiet, giving her space to express her grief. Her own eyes filled with tears, and when she glanced up, Alejandro was looking at her.

Melissa sniffled. "I'm sorry. This is so unexpected. I was happy we had found each other, and now he's gone. Foolish man. Do you know, the last time we talked, he mentioned giving me money because he didn't want to be a burden? I laughed it off, because how could my own flesh and blood be a burden? And where would he get money from? But now... do you think he was mixed up in something and didn't want to tell me?"

"If he was, I don't know anything about it."

"Why did this have to happen!" Melissa cried out. She sniffed again. "I'm sorry. I'm just... I don't know what to do right now."

"I understand your grief. I was excited for your reunion."

Melissa sighed. "What now?"

"I can pick up his stuff and have them ready for you tomorrow," Camila offered. "He also had a dog. He named her Poodle."

"He told me about Poodle. I'd love to have her."

"I'll get Poodle and his belongings for you today."

"Thank you." Melissa sighed heavily again. "I guess... I guess I'll have a different reason for being there tomorrow. I'll have to make arrangements for his body to be shipped back to California."

"The police will need you to identify the body. The lead detective, Detective Slater, is going to call you first thing in the morning."

"Would you come with me to the morgue? I don't think I can handle seeing him on my own."

"Of course, I'll come with you. Anything you need, let me know."

"Thank you, Camila, for everything. My brother's gone, but I'm glad we had the chance to talk to each other and get to know each other again. I guess he won't need the spare room after all." Her voice trembled and dimmed at the end.

They spoke for a few more minutes, finalizing the plans for the next day, and then Camila hung up.

"Are you okay?" Alejandro asked.

She shook her head. "I feel terrible for her. This was the first time I've used my connections to reunite family members, and it turned out horribly."

Alejandro came over and dropped to his haunches before her. "You did a good thing. You helped them find each other, and your work with other people in his situation is commendable. You do not have to volunteer at the shelter and shine a spotlight on these people, but you do, and I'm sure there are plenty of people who are appreciative of what you have done. People who never got the chance to say thank you."

"Thanks," Camila said softly.

He swiped away a tear hanging on her bottom lashes and splayed his fingers across her cheek. She leaned into the warmth of his touch. More than anything, she wanted to hide in his warm embrace, the same way she did when he came to visit after her mother's death. Resting in his strong arms had done wonders for soothing the ache of yet another loss.

When she lifted her gaze, he was so close, if she leaned forward a couple of inches, their mouths would touch. His gaze dropped to her lips, and she thought for sure he'd kiss her. Time suspended. She stopped breathing, her own gaze lowering to the temptation his mouth presented.

Then Alejandro shot to his feet, and the moment came to

an abrupt end. Camila swallowed her disappointment and sank deeper into the chair.

"Did she say anything that could give insight into Doug's mind before he passed?" Alejandro asked in an oddly gruff voice. He returned to the sofa.

"Um, not really, but she did say something which surprised me. She said Doug mentioned he would give her money because he didn't want to be a burden. I know he had a little money that he earned from collecting cans and metal, but... he didn't have real money. Why would he say something like that to his sister?"

"Could he have money that you were not aware of?"

"Possibly, but I feel as if I would have known, and from what Melissa said, she doesn't know where he could have gotten the funds from. Matter-of-fact, she dismissed the whole idea because she didn't need or want his money."

Alejandro hummed thoughtfully, his brow creasing in the way it did whenever he was in deep concentration.

"What did your boss say?" Camila asked.

"He's fine with me staying out here a little longer."

"Okay," Camila said, resting her hands on her thighs. "What do we do in the meantime?"

Alejandro stood. "In the meantime, you tell me everything you know about Alvaro and Javier Reyes."

"There's not much to tell, other than what I've already told you. Javier took over when his father retired."

"When was this?"

"About a year ago."

"Where is his father now?" Alejandro asked.

Camila shrugged. "Last I heard, he'd moved to Singapore. No one has seen him since his son took over the casinos."

"Is it possible that he's dead?"

"Dead?" She laughed. "No, he—"

Alejandro raised an eyebrow at her hesitation.

"I'm trying to figure out why Doug is dead, and now you're throwing Alvaro's death at me. This is nuts."

"I have seen lots of crazy behavior in my line of work. Nothing is off the table, especially where money is involved."

"You know, before Alvaro retired, there was a rumor that he didn't want his son to take over his casino empire. Everyone expected Alvaro's second in command—Patrick—to take over the businesses, but Javier was installed instead. Once he took over, he fired Patrick."

"Has he been doing a good job?"

"So far as I know. The Celestial Palace is one of the most popular casinos on the strip, and when the other one opens after the renovations are completed, it's expected to do well."

"But no one expected him to be the one to take the reins of the company," Alejandro said.

Camila shook her head.

"Something tells me that's going to become important later on. You mentioned going to pick up Doug's belongings for his sister?"

"Yes. I should go now."

~

ALEJANDRO WENT with Camila to pick up Doug's possessions, but he hung back until she introduced him to everyone.

"Where'd they find you? Hunks R Us?" Rhonda asked.

"Rhonda," Camila chided her.

Alejandro smiled, while the older woman laughed, a mischievous glint in her eyes that Camila had never seen before. Her behavior gave Camila a glimpse of what Rhonda's personality must have been like when she was younger and not in her current situation.

The older woman's smile died, and she pushed to her feet. "You heard about Doug?" she asked in her raspy voice.

Sadness came over Camila again. "Yes, I did. I guess you did too."

"We all did." She shook her head.

"His sister's coming tomorrow. Do all of these belong to him?" Camila pointed to the pile of bags stuffed with clothes and other items beside Rhonda.

Rhonda nodded. "Yes. I can't believe he's gone, but I kept an eye on everything for him."

"You knew him better than I did. Do you think he killed himself?" Camila asked.

"Is that what they're saying?" Rhonda asked in a shocked voice.

"Yes."

"Hell, no! Pardon my French. He wouldn't have left Poodle."

Camila bent and scratched behind the dog's ears.

"Cops probably shot him," Sam said, seated nearby.

"Nah, wasn't the cops," Rhonda said.

"Then who? Cause he sure as hell didn't kill himself," Sam mumbled.

"But what if he did?" Camila asked. "What if he was going through something none of us knew about?"

They all fell silent. No one had an answer but couldn't deny the possibility.

"Do you think anyone would have wanted to hurt him?" Alejandro asked.

Rhonda and Sam looked at each other.

"I can't think of any reason why anyone would, but you know how it is. Don't nobody want to acknowledge us, y'know what I mean?" Sam asked. "One of us go missing and don't nobody look for us or care. They treat us like we don't exist. Tommy been missing for six weeks, but who's looking for him? Not the cops. Now, putting a bullet in a man's head seems kinda extreme, if you ask me, but folks can be real mean."

Rhonda nodded. "Some people pick on us for kicks. Mean sons of bitches."

In her "Invisible Lives" series, homeless interviewees had shared disturbing stories that broke Camila's heart.

"I'll try to come back in a few days. If you think of anything, let me know," she said.

"We sure will. You doing okay?" Rhonda asked.

"As good as could be expected. I need a little time to process."

Rhonda nodded. "Oh, I almost forgot. This isn't all Doug's stuff. He had a locker at Heart & Mind. He paid for it in the past week."

Heart & Mind was a nonprofit that catered to the homeless. They offered a variety of services, including job training and placement, hygiene services such as showers and toiletries, transportation, and therapy sessions.

"Huh. I didn't know he had a locker. I'll let his sister know," Camila said.

Alejandro and Camila picked up Doug's belongings, including the dog, and headed to the car.

They settled the pup in the back seat and placed Doug's belongings in the trunk.

"I'm starving. How about some dinner?" Alejandro said.

"Great idea," Camila agreed. "I know the perfect place."

lejandro and Camila stopped by the pet store to pick up a dog bed and dog food. Their second stop was the store to pick up a few groceries, and then a small soul food restaurant popular with the locals. They placed their order to go and returned to her parents' house.

Instead of eating at the table, they ate in the living room. Poodle enthusiastically gobbled her dog food in a corner, while Camila sat cross-legged on the sofa with a Styrofoam container of grilled butterflied hotlinks, homestyle potatoes, steamed vegetables, and a biscuit.

Alejandro transferred his food to a plate and placed it on the coffee table—two grilled pork chops, macaroni and cheese, collard greens, and cornbread. "What time are we meeting Melissa tomorrow?" he asked.

"Ten-ish. She's driving from San Diego."

He placed a piece of pork chop in his mouth and moaned in disbelief as he chewed the tasty meat. "Damn, that's good."

"I've never had a bad meal from them. Sometimes the wait is long, but it's worth it." They ate quietly for a bit, and then Camila suddenly let out a laugh.

"What's so funny?" Alejandro asked.

"Thinking about Mommy and how she would kill us if she saw us eating in her living room on the good furniture."

Chuckling, Alejandro sliced off another piece of pork chop. "I remember that time when she threw her shoe at your father because he was eating pie in here."

"Oh my goodness, that's right! You were here that day. In his defense, he didn't know she was home, or he would have stayed in the den."

The den was the least liked room in the house because it only had one window and was therefore darker than other parts of the house.

"He found out very quickly."

"Yes, he did."

They both cracked up as they continued eating.

Moments later, Camila stared at her food. "I miss them so much," she whispered.

Every time she hurt, he hurt. Alejandro put down his knife and fork and rested a comforting hand on her upper back, rubbing his thumb back and forth across her spine.

In the past he'd come visit for a few days at a time. He couldn't tolerate much more before the cutting jealousy he felt toward Emilio overcame him. Then his friend died and after the funeral, guilt forced Alejandro to keep his distance.

He had been on assignment when her father passed, but when her mother passed, he was able to attend the funeral. Camila had been inconsolable, and he took off work for a couple of weeks to stay with her when Miguel returned to school.

After several days, he made her get out of bed and forced her to eat the food friends and family delivered on an almost daily basis. Staying at her parents' house, just the two of them, had transformed their relationship. The change had been subtle, but sure—unmistakable tension ramping up between them.

"I'm okay," Camila assured him with a faint smile.

Alejandro removed his hand.

"But I've made a decision," Camila continued. "After all this is over, I'm going to keep the house. I'm not ready to sell yet. Too many memories. Maybe I'll rent it out, make a little money for me and Miguel while someone else enjoys it for a while. When I'm ready, I'll discuss what to do next with him."

"Good plan," Alejandro said.

"I don't know if it's a good plan, but it'll work until I figure out what I want to do with the rest of my life. I'm sure you have your life all figured out." She placed her food on the table and closed the lid as if she'd lost her appetite.

"I am no different than you or anyone else. I'm figuring things out as I go," Alejandro said, breaking off a piece of cornbread and placing it in his mouth.

"You ever think you'll get married?" Camila asked tentatively, as if afraid to ask.

What a trick question. If he could, he would marry *her* in a minute. He'd decided long ago he didn't want anyone else—couldn't imagine spending the rest of his life with anyone else.

He'd had feelings for Camila since he was a teen, when every time he saw her, he wondered what her lips tasted like—or if he reached for her hand, how would she react? Would she hold his or pull away?

"Maybe. One day."

"You're really not seeing anyone seriously in Hopevale?"

"I'm not." He resumed eating.

"I'm surprised."

"Why?"

"I see the way women react to you, Alejandro. Look at how Rhonda behaved earlier."

"Older women like me for some reason."

"Must be your quiet intensity."

He wasn't looking at her when she made the statement and couldn't tell if she was kidding or not.

"I'm not kidding," she said, reading his mind. "What's the age of the oldest woman you've ever dated?"

"I don't think I want to tell you." He took a sip of lemonade.

"That old, huh?" Her smile took on its customary teasing edge.

"You need to mind your own business." He replaced the Styrofoam cup on the coffee table.

"Come on, tell me!" She shoved his arm.

"*Ay*," he said, pretending she hurt his arm.

Her eyes widened. "Is that the arm that got cut?"

"Yes, and it's still sore." He rubbed the spot, feeling the bandage underneath the sleeve of his shirt.

"I'm sorry, but I want an answer."

"You're not going to give up, are you?"

"Nope. You know once I set my mind to something—"

"You're like a dog with a bone."

"I prefer to say relentless or persistent, but I guess your answer works."

Alejandro sat back and watched her with his mouth tipped up at the corners. "When I tell you, you can't judge me."

"I promise not to judge." Camila crossed her heart.

He didn't answer right away just to torture her.

"Jandro!" she said in exasperation.

He chuckled. "Okay, okay, I'll tell you. She was fifty-five."

Her mouth fell open.

"You promised not to judge," he reminded her, pointing a finger in her face.

She closed her mouth. "I'm not judging."

He glared at her and then ate some of his macaroni and cheese.

"You're thirty-four years old, which means your girlfriend was twenty-one years older than you."

"She was not my girlfriend, and we were involved two years ago, which means she was twenty-three years older than me."

"You like older women?" she asked.

"I like women. By the way, she was a young fifty-five."

"Whatever that means."

"It means she could keep up with me, smart ass."

"And what does that mean?" she asked, her voice dropping unusually low.

He wiped his mouth with his napkin and placed it on the table with a deliberate movement. "You know what it means."

There was a pulse of silence before she lowered her gaze and faint color tinged her cheeks. "Oh."

That color let him know he was having an effect on her. *Interesting.* He should stop, but he was a selfish SOB who wanted inside of her in a way he had never wanted another woman.

He stretched an arm across the top of the sofa, inches from touching her. "What about you? Do you think you'll remarry?"

His gaze traveled from her face down to the swell of her breasts, his molars grinding against each other in jealousy at the mere thought of some future man having what he couldn't.

Camila shrugged. "Don't know. Like you, maybe one day. I'm not seeing anyone seriously at the moment, so I haven't thought about it much."

"Any man would be lucky to have you. I mean that."

This conversation had turned into foreplay, and a familiar feeling came over him—one he knew all too well. Arousal. Climbing the inside of his thighs and resting behind the fly of his jeans.

"Any woman would be lucky to have *you*. You're a good guy."

He arched an eyebrow. If only she knew, he was a man with a dark heart, capable of anything.

"You *are*," she insisted. "You saved my life last night, and in case I forgot to tell you, thank you."

"You're welcome. I would do it again."

"Which is why you're a good guy," Camila said softly.

She was killing him with her soft voice and her eyes looking at him with—what? Hero worship? No. There was something else in her eyes.

He wound some of her hair around his fingers, testing the waters. "I haven't been called good very often," he said huskily. He gently tugged her hair, and her breath caught, a hint of surprise and excitement entering her eyes.

This was new and dangerous territory for them, but he wanted her. Oh, how he'd wanted her for ages. He leaned closer, his manhood swelling inside his boxers.

She licked her lips, turning them shiny and temptingly moist.

Alejandro took her hand and placed her palm over the bulge in his pants. She gasped and dropped her gaze. The message was clear. He wasn't playing a game. His intention was to fuck her. To take his pleasure between her thighs and give as many orgasms as she could tolerate.

He leaned closer again to finally have the pleasure of tasting her lips. They were so close to each other he could practically feel the sparks jumping the short distance between them.

At that exact moment, Poodle lifted her front paws onto the sofa and barked. Alejandro had completely forgotten the damn dog was in the house.

Camila jumped back, snapping out of the trance that had ensnared them both. Her cheeks flushed. "I..." She looked shell-shocked, as if she didn't understand what had happened.

A spasm of pain twisted inside his chest. "Camila—"

She shot to her feet when he reached for her and looked at

him as if she didn't know him. Her rejection landed like an uppercut to the chin. Sudden, dizzying, brutal.

Slowly, Alejandro stood, and she picked up the dog, holding her close like a protective shield. "I-I don't think..."

"Understood," he said, saving her from further explanation.

"I'm going upstairs."

"I will clean up."

Their voices sounded stilted and unnatural, normal conversation acutely *ab*normal in the wake of such a peculiar interaction between them.

"Thanks." She backed away and hurried from the room, rushing up the stairs with the dog in her arms.

Alejandro remained in the same spot for too long, reliving the warmth of her hand on him. He couldn't stop thinking about her touch and was hard to the point of pain.

When he finally moved, he cleaned up the living room and walked up into the kitchen to place the leftover food in the refrigerator. The entire time he silently cursed himself for his behavior. He hadn't misread her feelings, but clearly she didn't want to feel desire for him—and definitely not act on it.

He had screwed up in a big way. For so long he had mastered the art of hiding her effect on him. Tonight the mask had slipped.

Because of his own selfish needs, he might have damaged their relationship for good.

13

The following day, Camila and Alejandro drove to the ME's office to meet Melissa. She had called to let them know she talked to the detective on the drive up, and he explained she could go in to identify her brother.

On the ride there, the Honda seemed especially small. All Camila could think about was the almost-kiss between her and Alejandro the night before. He had been aroused. *Very* aroused. The impression of his hard-on was branded into her hand, and he was *huge*.

Getting ready this morning had been awkward as they moved around the kitchen, both of them careful not to touch. Which was almost impossible because of his size. A man almost six foot three with broad shoulders took up a lot of space. The air around them had been strained—which reminded her of how she had felt when he stayed with her after her mother's funeral.

An underlying... tension emerged between them during those two weeks, though neither of them acknowledged it. The feeling was so powerful, she almost suffocated. She hadn't wanted him to go but was happy when he left so she could breathe again.

The feeling had returned. Stronger. More powerful. A hand covering her nose and mouth.

She didn't know how to explain why she had reacted the way she did, except to say the sexual tension between them had been unexpected, and despite wanting him, fear held her back.

Fear of what he would do when he learned the truth—that she wasn't sweet and perfect like he believed. Because she was the reason Emilio was dead.

Staring out the window, she clenched her hands in her lap, swallowing hard at the painful memory and vowing to stifle her emotions. To pretend. Pretend nothing had changed and the more than twenty years of pent-up feelings didn't exist. Otherwise, she would lose her mind.

Alejandro parked the car in the shade of a tree at the end of the lot and stepped out holding Poodle in his arms. As if he wasn't already sexy, seeing him holding the pup made him even more so. Why was it that big, brawny men holding small animals was so attractive?

Melissa approached them, a small woman with wiry blonde hair that barely touched her shoulders. As a testament to the toughness of life on the street, she looked at least ten years younger than her brother, though she was the elder sibling.

Her eyes were dry but red-rimmed, as if she'd cried on her way there, but she smiled when she saw the dog. "Is that Poodle?" she cooed.

"This is her," Camila confirmed.

While Melissa scratched behind the terrier's ear, the dog remained nestled in Alejandro's beefy arms, thoroughly satisfied by all the attention she was receiving.

Finally, Melissa took a deep breath and placed an obviously forced smile on her lips. "You must be Alejandro," she said.

"I am. Nice to meet you."

"How are you holding up?" Camila asked.

"I'm here," Melissa replied.

Camila placed a comforting hand on her shoulder. "Alejandro's going to wait here with Poodle while you and I go inside to see the body. Ready?"

"Ready," Melissa answered, barely above a whisper.

Camila took her hand, and they entered the building together. Although she barely knew the other woman, she felt close to her because they had lost Doug in such an unexpected way.

Inside, they met Vicky, the coroner's assistant. Tall, with her black hair held back by a colorful scarf, she warned them about the condition of Doug's appearance. Despite the warning, Camila quietly gasped when she saw the right side of his face blown off. Melissa put a hand over her mouth and whimpered, tears filling her eyes.

Camila had been hoping for a miracle, but... no doubt about it—that was Doug lying on the cold metal table.

After their confirmation, Vicky rolled the sheet over his face again, and Melissa excused herself to rush from the room. Though disturbed by what she had seen, Camila didn't leave right away.

"Did you say the medical examiner decided this was suicide?" she asked.

"Yes, he was shot in the side of the head, as you can see."

"I'm sorry, but there's no way he killed himself. Holding a gun to the right side of his head would be impossible for Doug. He had an old army injury, which made it impossible for him to lift his hand higher than a forty-five degree angle. He couldn't have shot himself."

Frowning, Vicky looked down at her paperwork. "I'm sorry, but that's what Dr. Stenner determined." She looked up again.

"Is there any way I can talk to him?"

"I suppose so. He'll be here tomorrow. You can call and make an appointment."

"If he could see me first thing in the morning, I'd appreciate it."

She smiled. "I'll let him know you'll be here when the office opens."

"Thank you."

Camila exited the room and found Melissa in the bathroom.

"That was... horrible," Melissa said.

"Way worse than I expected," Camila agreed.

Melissa sniffled. "Thank you for coming with me. I couldn't have done it alone." Melissa dabbed her nose with tissue.

Camila slipped an arm around her shoulders. "You don't have to thank me. I was happy to do it. Doug was a friend of mine, and I can't believe he's gone."

"Me either."

They walked slowly toward the front of the building. As they strolled into the sunshine, Melissa squinted and cleared her throat. "You brought his things with you?"

"They're in the trunk."

They returned to where Alejandro was leaning against the car with Poodle in his arms. He looked like an advertisement for a fireman's calendar—holding an adorable dog, with his tattooed arms exposed by the cut-off sleeves of a close-fitting T-shirt.

"She's ready to take his things. Would you pop the trunk?" Camila asked, not quite able to meet his gaze.

Alejandro moved Doug's belongings into Melissa's rental while she held the dog in her arms. She licked Melissa's chin, and she laughed.

"You know, I've never been much of a pet person, but Poodle might force me to make an exception."

"She's a well-behaved dog," Camila said.

"Doug chose well."

"Yes, he did," Camila agreed.

When Alejandro finished transferring Doug's possessions, Camila turned to Melissa. "Next stop is Heart & Mind. I notified the manager and she's expecting us. She said she'll let you take whatever is in Doug's locker."

"I'm ready."

"You can follow behind us, but here's the address just in case." She handed Melissa a slip of paper.

"Got it. I'll meet you there." Holding on to Poodle, she walked to her car.

Camila and Alejandro climbed in their vehicle and pulled out of the lot.

"How is she?" Alejandro asked.

"She took it hard," Camila answered, explaining Doug's appearance and how Melissa had rushed to the bathroom. "Something's not adding up though. Doug was shot on the right side of his face, but there's no way he could have committed suicide in that way." She explained about his injury.

"Which means what you suspected is true. He didn't kill himself."

"I'm one hundred percent certain now, and I told the coroner's assistant I'd like to speak to Dr. Stenner in the morning. He wasn't there today." She paused, thinking. "If Doug didn't kill himself, why does someone want people to think he did?" Camila asked.

"The million dollar question. Are you going to tell Melissa?"

She gnawed her bottom lip. "I haven't decided yet. Not now, anyway. Not until after I talk to Dr. Stenner."

They both fell silent and didn't speak much for the rest of the ride over, except for her to give directions to Heart & Mind. Seconds after they arrived, Melissa pulled up behind them.

"Be right back." Camila hopped out of the vehicle.

She and Melissa went inside, leaving Poodle with Alejandro

again. Right away, Camila saw MacKenzie, the manager of the nonprofit.

"Camila! How are you?" She had a bunch of mail in her arms, her brunette hair in a sleek ponytail.

"Hi, how's it going? This is Doug's sister, Melissa. Melissa, this is MacKenzie. She runs this place."

MacKenzie's eyes softened. "I'm so sorry for your loss."

"Thank you," Melissa said gratefully.

"Doug was a good guy. We once had someone come in here acting crazy, yelling, and carrying on. Doug calmed him down and made sure he knew he needed to respect us and the work we do. Makes sense since he used to be military police. He'll be missed."

"I want to hear all the stories about my brother. Sounds like he was exactly the same as when we were kids—always looking out for everyone else."

"He definitely was. Let me get the key."

MacKenzie left them standing in the lobby and returned moments later.

"Rhonda said he's only had this locker for about a week. Is that right?" Camila asked.

"That's right. He came in last week, after he'd scraped up the money to pay for the space. He said he had something valuable he wanted to keep in there. This is the key. His locker is all the way down at the end, at the top."

"Thanks, MacKenzie."

"Not a problem. I know you and Doug were close. You're doing great work, Camila."

"I try. We'll bring back the key as soon as we're finished."

"Hand it to Aaron when you're finished if you don't see me. I have some work to do in the back."

"Will do."

Camila and Melissa went in the direction of the lockers, which were all located in a room off from the lobby. The room was dark, but when they entered, the lights flickered on.

Following MacKenzie's instructions, they walked to the end. Camila handed over the key, and Melissa inserted it into the lock. With a right twist and a pull, the door opened.

Looking over the other woman's shoulder, Camila saw a slightly dirty white 9 X 12 envelope and a stack of papers.

"Doesn't look like much," Melissa remarked, taking everything out. "Oh, this is weird."

The papers appeared to have been shredded then taped back together.

"These are from the clinic." Camila pointed to the name at the top—Community Care Center.

"Why would he have shredded documents from the clinic?" Melissa asked.

"Don't know. Mind if I take a look at them?"

"No, go right ahead." Melissa handed her the documents and made her way out the locker room. When they didn't see MacKenzie, she handed the key to Aaron as instructed and then left.

Alejandro's eyes followed them as they approached. "What did you find?" he asked.

"Files from Community Care Center, Dr. Shapiro's clinic."

Melissa tore open the envelope and pulled out a stack of photos. "Huh. Doug had a camera?"

"I bought him a disposable one because he wanted to take photos of Vegas and his friends before he left for California," Camila said.

They flipped through the images. Mostly they were of other homeless people, like Rhonda and Sam. There were photos of Las Vegas at various times during the day, including at night, and a couple of shots of Camila and Doug.

"You should keep one of these." Melissa handed her one of the photos.

"Thank you."

Suddenly, Melissa stopped. "Do you know who this is?"

Camila peered at the photo in shock. *What the hell?* "That's Dr. Shapiro and Javier Reyes," she said slowly.

"Since you know them, you can have these. There are three photos of both men."

Melissa handed them over, and Camila examined the pictures. Reyes's limo was parked in front of the clinic at night, and both men stood outside near the door, in what looked like a heated conversation. In one of the photos, Reyes had jabbed his finger in Dr. Shapiro's chest.

Melissa lifted Poodle from Alejandro's arms. "I guess that's it for me. I have to make arrangements for Doug's body to be transported to California. Then I'm headed home."

Camila squeezed her arm. "I'll check on you in a few days. If you need anything, don't hesitate to call."

"You do the same. If not for you, I wouldn't have found my brother. Although he passed before we could reestablish our relationship in person, I'm forever indebted to you."

Both women hugged, and Camila petted Poodle's head one more time before Melissa said goodbye to her and Alejandro and climbed into her rental.

After she had driven off, Camila turned to Alejandro. "What do you make of these photos?" She showed him the three of Shapiro and Reyes.

He frowned down at the images. "Looks like they're having an interesting conversation."

"Yes, it does. I don't understand any of this. Everybody loves Dr. Shapiro. Why would he be involved with a scumbag like Reyes? What are they arguing about, and could these pictures be why Doug is dead?"

"It's possible."

Camila held up the papers in her hand. "We need to

examine these documents. I only briefly reviewed them, but I think these, along with the photos, are why Doug called me."

"Reyes must have known he called you. Maybe he also knew he had these files or took the photos—or both. Do you know if the police found the prepaid phone Doug's sister bought for him?"

Camila shook her head. "I don't know, and I didn't think to ask Detective Slater, but I can find out tomorrow. I can give him a call or reach out to a source I have in the police department."

"Contact your friend. I'm not convinced you can trust the detective."

He was probably right.

"What's going on here, Alejandro?"

"I don't know, but whatever it is, I have no doubt Reyes is willing to kill to keep the secret."

14

"These are the forms they use for non-paying patients," Camila said, flipping through the taped together sheets.

Alejandro sat opposite her in her parents' living room, the three photos spread out on the coffee table between them. There were ten sheets of paper, and he reviewed five while she reviewed the other five.

"They don't contain much information," he remarked.

"It's an intake form," Camila explained. "To collect basic information from patients and give medical personnel an idea of why they came in. I haven't been down to the clinic in a while, but on the fee-free Saturdays they ran, I used to help people fill out this form because some of them couldn't read and needed help answering the questions. Mommy went with me a few times and helped."

"How would Doug have gotten this information?" Alejandro asked.

"Dumpster diving, probably."

Alejandro leaned back on the sofa. "Seems like an odd

place to dumpster dive, no? A clinic? Why not the back of the casinos or a restaurant?"

"He probably rummaged through those dumpsters too."

Alejandro stroked his jaw as he thought. "What could he have been looking for at the clinic?"

"What do you mean?"

He pointed at the photographs. "There is a reason he took these."

Camila stood, and with one hand on her hip started pacing the floor. "We know Reyes is a crook. Doug could have suspected something was going on—maybe he was threatening Dr. Shapiro—which could explain why Doug took the photos. The voicemail he left said he had something for me, which could be all of this. He probably thought I could do some digging for him."

Alejandro studied the photographs for a moment. "In one of the photos, yes, Javier is in the doctor's face, but in the other two, they are having a heated conversation. Look at their expressions. They both look concerned. Worried." He flipped the pictures upside down so they were facing right side up in her direction.

"Worried about what, though?"

"Good question."

He looked at a different clinic sheet and reviewed every line in detail. Nothing stood out to him. The questions seemed normal.

Do you smoke or use tobacco? How much?

How much alcohol do you consume?

Do you have hepatitis, HIV/AIDS?

Have you ever had any serious illnesses or chronic conditions (e.g., diabetes, cancer, heart disease, kidney disease, etc.)?

He continued reading, but when he arrived at the bottom, a chill came over him. In the box marked *office use only*, someone had written a note.

Viable organs: kidneys, pancreas

"Camila, do you see notes at the bottom of your sheets? In the *office use only* section?"

She picked up her papers. "Why?"

Alejandro didn't answer. He let her review them first.

She sifted through the papers. "Not on this one... oh, there's something written at the bottom of two of them. *Viable organs: all. Viable organs: liver, kidneys.*" She looked up at him. "What does that mean?"

"You know what it means," Alejandro said softly.

"Wait a minute, are you suggesting the clinic is-is taking *organs* from the patients?"

Instead of answering, Alejandro showed her his last sheet. He pointed to the name at the top. "What was the name of the homeless man Sam and Rhonda said has been missing for six weeks?"

Camila read the name. "Tommy," she whispered. She sank into the armchair.

"Sam said no one cared or was looking for Tommy, but what if Doug was? What if he suspected something was going on or knew something was wrong?"

"That would explain why he was searching through the dumpster at the clinic. Then he actually did find something. Oh my goodness, if he figured out what was going on, he might have confronted Dr. Shapiro. Melissa said he was coming into some money and wanted to help out."

"He could have tried to blackmail him."

Camila fell back against the chair and covered her face with her hands. "No, no, no, Doug, what did you do?"

A knock came at the door.

"Lunch," Alejandro said. He went to the door, paid the delivery person, and took the Chinese food up the three steps into the kitchen.

Camila followed him, bringing her laptop. She sat at the

bar. "I'm going to do a little digging and see if I can figure out the connection between Shapiro and Reyes." Her fingers moved quickly across the keyboard.

"How are you going to do that?" Alejandro asked, setting out plates.

"Because of *Sin City Pulse*, I have access to different databases. I just need to cross reference their names and see what comes up." She was typing fast, not looking at him as she spoke.

Alejandro fixed them each a plate of kung pao chicken and orange chicken with rice and an egg roll.

He ate while Camila barely touched her food as she scrolled through pages upon pages of data. She was in the zone, excited by the search she was conducting. Her dogged determination to find a link between both men was certainly a good characteristic to have as a local reporter.

When Alejandro finished eating, he went back to the photos and the intake forms. He used a highlighter on six of the sheets that indicated the patients had viable organs. Then he did some online digging to get general information on black market organ transplants.

Several hours had passed by the time he heard Camila gasp. "I found something," she said from the kitchen.

Alejandro went to stand behind her.

"Look at this," she said, pointing at the screen. "I couldn't find a direct link between them, but they both attended Alexander Academy. It's an expensive private school where the wealthy and celebrities send their kids. Shapiro attended on scholarship. Then, they both went to Berkeley. Javier came back to Vegas after graduation while Shapiro went on to med school. Of course, this doesn't mean they knew each other, but..." She looked at him hopefully.

"I do not think it's a coincidence," Alejandro said.

"I don't, either. Here's something else." She clicked on another tab. "Apparently, Dr. Shapiro goes to Tijuana pretty regularly. According to this article, he says he visits once a month to provide services at a clinic he opened there, offering the same oxygen therapy treatments." She clicked on another tab. "Javier has a house in Tijuana."

"Another coincidence." Alejandro paced away from her. "Unfortunately, all we have are coincidences. Even the intake forms don't mean anything. They are not incriminating by themselves. Dr. Shapiro and his staff more than likely have a very logical explanation for why they were testing patients' organs for viability."

Camila spun on the stool to face him. "We'd have to get something concrete on them. I mean, where are these patients? We know for sure Tommy is missing, but what about the others, and what percentage of the clinic's patients go missing?"

Alejandro nodded slowly, looking at her as an idea formulated in his mind. "We could go to Tijuana." When she looked surprised, he continued. "It's a top medical tourism destination. If they are harvesting here, they are taking a big risk, so they are less likely to turn it into a full-fledged operation. Besides, if Doug uncovered what they were doing, they would have locked down tight in Vegas. They might have stopped altogether. In Tijuana, their guard will be down, and what better place to hide their operation than among all the reputable medical businesses?"

"Makes sense, but what would we do while we're there?"

"We go to Tijuana, maybe pretend one of us needs oxygen therapy so we can look around the facility. We might be able to get incriminating evidence on Reyes and Shapiro. I have a friend who's a taxi driver down there. I could make a call and have him meet us."

Her lips puckered in a resolute way. "I'm game if you are. How soon do you want to go?"

"Right away. If these men are doing what we think they are, I want to stop them immediately and keep other people from getting hurt. Let me make a call, and in the meantime, you need to eat something."

Camila wrinkled her nose. "My food is cold now."

"That's what microwaves are for. Take a break, and I will call my friend." Alejandro returned to the living room and picked up his phone.

15

Alejandro returned to the kitchen after his conversation with his contact in Tijuana. "I talked to my friend, and he's available to meet us tomorrow. He'll also do some checking to see what he can find out about Shapiro's clinic down there."

Camila sat at the bar eating her food and paused with a forkful of rice halfway to her mouth. "What time do you want to go? Maybe right after the coroner's visit?" she suggested.

"That's a good idea since it's a six-hour flight. I'll see if there are any seats available. I'll pay for the tickets." He opened her laptop.

"You don't have to do that," Camila said, sounding appalled.

"I don't mind." Alejandro typed in a search for flights.

"I can pay for my own ticket."

"I can pay for your ticket too," he said, flicking a look at her before returning his attention to the computer.

They spent the next few moments discussing the best time to go and settled on early afternoon. Seats were available but not together. Alejandro paid for the tickets and then tucked his card back into his wallet. "All done," he said, closing the laptop.

"Thanks," Camila said.

Alejandro got a Negra Modelo beer from the refrigerator and popped it open. The entire time he could feel Camila's eyes on him.

"We should—"

"I'm going to—"

They both spoke at the same time and stopped, laughing a little. Without the urgency of the investigation to occupy them, the awkwardness had returned.

"You go first," Alejandro said.

Camila took a deep breath and set down her fork. "We need to talk."

Mierda. "About what?"

"I can already see your guard is up."

"It's rarely a good thing when a woman says, 'we need to talk.'"

"That's fair." She shifted on the stool. "I, uh, want to talk about last night."

He tensed but didn't say a word, holding the cold beer in his hand as he waited to hear what else she had to say.

Camila cleared her throat. "Today there's been awkward-ness between us because of what happened, and—"

"What happened last night should not have happened. I should not have made a pass at you. I wasn't thinking. We can forget about it."

"I don't want to forget about it. I want to explain my reac-tion, please. I didn't reject you. I didn't know how to respond because you and I have never been in a situation like that before."

"I put us in that position, and I'm sorry—"

"Don't apologize!" Camila snapped. "Listen to what I'm saying, Jandro. What happened was unusual for us, and we should discuss what it means."

"What it means?"

"Yes! Do you have feelings? Are you human?" she asked.

How ironic for her to ask such a question, when she was one of the few people he lowered his guard for because doing so was discouraged in his line of work.

"Of course I have feelings," he said, though he felt himself shutting down.

"I know I sound emotional, but not everyone is a machine like you. We can't all compartmentalize. I mean, I know you care. You were always there for me and Emilio. Keeping bullies away from him, and you've always had my back, and to this day help me with... life. But when Emilio died, a change happened, and I can't quite put my finger on what it was. *Everything* changed. Seems like he was the glue holding us together. Was he?" Her question came out tentative and unsure.

"It's understandable that we struggled. I lost my friend and you lost your husband."

In retrospect, Emilio's death left them broken and unsure of how to continue. The dynamics of their friendship had changed. Instead of three, now there were only two of them.

"You and he were closer. You both lived in Jalisco, and I was only there during the summers."

"You were closer. You were his on-and-off girlfriend for years. He moved to this country because of you. You married here. He and I..." He shook his head. "We were friends, but you were his soulmate." The word grated across his tongue like rough sandpaper.

"And how did you feel about me?"

He refused to look at her or she'd know without a doubt his feelings for her had long surpassed friendship. Gripping the bottle, he said, "You were my friend too."

"What changed last night?"

"I don't know, Camila! We grew up. You are a beautiful woman. I am a man."

She looked at him with baleful brown eyes. "I'm never going to see you again after this, am I?" she asked.

Alejandro expelled a heavy breath from his lungs. "You said yourself that our relationship has changed. We're not comfortable around each other anymore, and maybe it's best we keep our distance after I return to Georgia. We will go to Tijuana and see what we can find out about Dr. Shapiro's clinic, and if we're lucky, we'll gather enough information to prove what we already know—that they are harvesting organs." A perfectly reasonable but ridiculous decision if he ever heard one.

Camila's lips tightened. "Great." She got down off the stool, scraped her leftover food into the trash, and tossed the dishes in the sink with a clatter.

"What do you want me to say?"

"Nothing," she answered with an abundance of snark. "I don't expect anything from you. Why would I expect anything from a man who said goodbye at seventeen and didn't show up again until almost three years later?"

"You know why," Alejandro grated.

"Then you spent the last fourteen years popping in and out of my life—disappearing for months at a time with 'top-secret government work,' as an excuse," she said, adding bass to her voice to mimic his tone.

"Did you think I was lying about my work?"

"I don't know, were you?"

"No, Camila. I really did work for the government. I killed two men in your house, remember?"

"Maybe you're a criminal, like Detective Slater said."

Antarctic chill descended on the room.

"Like my parents. Is that what you're implying?" he asked in a cool voice.

"I didn't say a word about your parents or your past."

"But you want to."

"I do *not*." She threw up her hands in frustration. "You know what, forget it. I tried. For some reason, you want to make me into the bad guy. God forbid we open up to each other and share. That's the difference between you and—"

She stopped abruptly, her lips went tight again, and Alejandro's entire body became rigid.

He narrowed his eyes. "Me and who?" he asked in a lethally low voice. He knew the answer but wanted to force her to say the name.

"No one."

"Finish the fucking sentence."

She glared at him. "Don't curse at me."

"Then finish the sentence!" He slammed his fist on the bar.

"That's the difference between you and Emilio!' she yelled.

The words were a slap in the face. He didn't know what to do with the emotion surging through him.

"You feel better now?" he asked.

"You asked. You insisted I tell you." She was breathing hard. He saw a hint of regret in her eyes, but she refused to back down.

"No, you wanted to tell me, *querida*. Emilio, the son of the priest, the good guy. Meanwhile, I am the son of criminals, the bad guy. Tell the truth, you have been wanting to talk about our differences for a long time, haven't you?"

She shook her head. "Not the way you think."

"No? Isn't that why you married him? Because he is a good man. Because he talks and I don't?"

"That's not why I married him."

"Well, you didn't marry me, *querida*, and no man has ever been as close to you as me and Emilio. So why did you marry him? Hmm?"

She stared at him in silence. When she didn't answer, Alejandro leaned across the bar. "Who is the one who will not talk now?"

He shoved away. He needed to get out of this house. Out of

this city. He shouldn't have agreed to come here. He should have sent a wedding gift like a smart person instead of subjecting himself to this bullshit.

"He asked!" Her voice quivered on those two words and halted his feet on the steps. "He said he wanted to take care of me. He told me that he'd loved me since we were kids."

I've loved you since we were kids! Alejandro bellowed on the inside.

She wasn't done. "He said every time we broke up over the years, a piece of him died. He missed me. He needed me. He said the most beautiful words and shared his feelings. And... and he asked me to marry him, Alejandro."

He left then, charging through the front door and slamming it so hard he was certain the entire house shook. He could almost hear the next sentence at the end of her speech.

You never asked.

He had never asked because he thought she could do better. Because she had chosen Emilio. Because Emilio was his friend, and what kind of lowlife would move in on his friend's woman?

Looking down, he realized he held the beer bottle in his hand. He tipped his head back and drained it in two gulps.

She had belonged to Emilio. Simple. And Emilio had loved her with all his heart. Each time they broke up, he called Alejandro to tell him of his misery. Like a fool he'd give him advice and tell him how to win her back. Or tell him to be patient and give her time.

They always reconciled. Then they married and were together for five years before his death. As far as Alejandro knew, they had been happy. Once she became his wife, his friend never complained about her again. Why would he? He had won the greatest prize of all.

Her heart.

16

C amila stepped out of the shower and dried off. Since Alejandro stormed out, she hadn't been able to think about anything but their argument. Maybe she had said too much, but there was so much more she wanted to say. So much he didn't know.

She wiped the condensation off the mirror and stared at her reflection. She was sorry they'd argued, but she wasn't sorry about what she'd said. For so long she'd held in her feelings, and it was time for her to let them out. He had clearly needed to get a few things off his chest too. How their words would affect their relationship moving forward remained to be seen.

She laughed softly and without mirth. Actually, he'd been clear they wouldn't have much of a relationship after he left, as if she hadn't already been suffering from lack of contact.

She pulled the shower cap off her head and let her hair fall onto her shoulders and down her back. Then she covered her body in moisturizing, pineapple-and honey-scented lotion. She re-wrapped her body in the towel and walked into the bedroom.

She pulled up short when she saw Alejandro sitting on the

end of the bed. He moved so quietly, she hadn't heard him come in. When did he come back and how long had he been sitting there? He still looked angry, but his broad shoulders were rounded, as if the fight had gone out of him.

"What would you have said, if I had asked you to marry me?" he asked, his voice low and deeper than she'd ever heard it.

Camila licked her dry lips, her heart racing two times faster than normal. "I would have said yes," she answered in a whisper.

Neither of them moved for the longest time. They simply stared at each other. Did he care? Did her answer matter? Did he understand she was baring her soul to him without any guarantee he would reciprocate her feelings?

Finally, Alejandro came to his feet and walked slowly over to where she stood. He swallowed hard, his face twisting with pain. He caged her head in his big hands.

"If I had known—if I had known, Camila, I swear I would have done everything differently. *Fuck*. Months would not have gone by without you seeing me. I love you. I love you so goddamn much. I have loved you for as long as I can remember. I think I fell in love with you that very first day, when you said *hola* and handed me the flower."

Tears filled her eyes and caused his face to blur. "Jandro... I wish..." Her voice cracked. Overcome with emotion, she couldn't continue, but no more words were needed.

He bent his head and kissed away the tears streaming from the corner of her eyes and onto her cheeks. His lips on her skin were a welcome balm, soothing the ache from all the years they had hidden their feelings from each other. He pulled her closer, and she melted into him, their hearts beating in sync, unshackled from the doubt, fear, and insecurity that had kept them apart.

Clutching his shirt, she lifted her lips, and right away the fingers of one hand tunneled into her hair and his mouth seized hers.

Finally. Yearning unfurled in the pit of her stomach.

The kiss was chaotic and urgent. Alejandro slid his tongue along the seam of her lips, and she parted them with a gasp, allowing his tongue to plunder her mouth and eagerly explore.

Heart pounding in her chest, her world narrowed to the pressure of his mouth moving against hers—firm, demanding, yet tender. She savored his masculine flavor blended with the sharp taste of the dark beer. The heat between them built quickly, spreading through her body with the speed of an explosion. Beneath her fingertips, his heart beat in the same rapid staccato as her own.

Time stopped. The kiss was everything she had imagined and more. She was lost in it, in him, unable to remember a time when she hadn't wanted or needed this.

His taste was intoxicating, flooding her senses until nothing else mattered. Nothing but their mouths seared together, his one hand clenched in her hair while the other pressed her flush against his hard body. Her knees weakened as she clung to him, fingers tightening in his shirt as if letting go would cause her to lose her balance and this moment.

There was a desperation in the way Alejandro kissed her, as if he, too, had been waiting for this—aching for it—just as much as she had been. The way he held her, the way he kissed her, was a confession.

She ran her hands over his chest. His body was composed of solid muscle. She pushed his shirt higher, letting her fingertips trace the ridges of his abdomen. Touching his flesh was intoxicating and arousing. All these years, every time she'd touched him had been in friendship. This was sexual, and her brain was short-circuiting.

"I want you naked," he husked in her ear.

She helped him remove his clothes, barely managing not to

tear them to shreds. Transfixed by the beauty of his naked body, all Camila could do was stare. Broad shoulders flanked a tight, muscular chest that narrowed around lean hips to cradle a— *wow*—she caught her breath at the sight of his jutting erection nestled in the hairs between his thighs.

She dropped her towel to the floor before they fell onto the bed in a tangle of naked arms and legs. His lips found her neck, and his long fingers cradled her behind.

"You have such a beautiful ass. I could look at it all day," he whispered.

"That can be arranged."

"Don't tease me."

Leaning over her on one elbow, Alejandro kissed his way down her shoulder, at the same time allowing his hand to trace the curves of her body. Down her side and over the flat plane of her stomach.

Then his mouth moved lower, warm and moist, his tongue flicking against her heated skin. He hovered above her erect nipple, letting his breath tease the taut peak. Camila sucked in a deep breath that transformed into a moan of frustration at his unbelievable self-control.

Why didn't he take the nipple into his mouth? Why didn't he put her out of her misery?

Straining upward, she grabbed the back of his head and forced her breast into his mouth. His lips closed around her dark flesh as he sucked and teased the tight bud with his tongue.

Sharp pleasure arrowed to her groin as her head started spinning. She had known his touch would be enjoyable, but this—this was otherworldly good.

His hand slid between her thighs and stroked her slick heat. A mewl of satisfaction escaped her lips as she arched her spine and clutched the back of his head, her fingers sinking into the softness of his black hair.

Noting her reaction to his lovemaking, Alejandro continued to suck and lick, going from one breast to the other. Driving her crazy with each delicious swipe of his tongue and tug of his lips.

She held fast to him and strained closer, working her hips against his hand, and slowly spiraling out of control, as the hairs on his chiseled chest teased her nipples and added to the pleasurable sensations dominating her senses.

He kissed her again. This time with more urgency. He ravaged her—his tongue plundering her mouth and drawing moan after moan from the depths of her throat.

His muscular body pressed down on top of hers, his hard dick between her legs a straight, impatient rod bumping her tender core.

Past hurts disappeared. Nothing else mattered but the two of them in this very moment. In this time. Together at last.

Camila explored his body with relish. He was magnificent. A warrior. But when she saw the bluish-purple bruises on his back, she sucked in a breath of horror. A wave of guilt crashed over her, and her throat tightened with the weight of an unspoken apology, knowing every bruise was because of her.

"Alejandro," she whispered. She kissed the first mark and felt a tremor run through him. Each time her lips touched skin, his muscles twitched.

Their movements became more frantic. They twisted and turned on the mattress, limbs tangling in the sheets as they caressed and kissed with urgency. She moved restlessly beneath his big body, enjoying every touch of his hand, the earthy scent of his skin, and the hard, roughened texture of his body against hers.

When he curled his fingers beneath her bottom, she immediately spread her legs. Ready. Panting. Anxious to receive him.

The tip of his erection pushed against her, and she whimpered with anticipation.

She wanted him. Needed him like no other.

"Jandro, please. *Please*," she begged without shame. She just needed him so desperately.

Moist heat spread between her thighs as her desire increased, and they locked eyes while he slid his body inside hers. Right before she closed her eyes, he grimaced and closed his eyes, and they both released a low moan.

Camila's arms tightened around his neck as she urged him to move.

When he did, his thrusts were hard and deep, his hands angling her hips higher to give him more control. She tossed back her head and let loose a cry of unbridled passion. Too much. *Oh god.* He was too much. She could hardly breathe from the pleasure.

Finally, she belonged to him. Finally, he belonged to her. No barriers between them. Skin to skin. She was in the arms of the man she'd loved for a lifetime.

Her friend. Her protector.

And now, her lover.

Over and over, Alejandro withdrew and then filled her with his swollen, rigid flesh. Driving her mindless. Nothing had ever felt this good.

Suddenly, he stopped and flipped her over. Then he was inside her again, and the pressure was so delicious from that position that her mouth opened on a soft gasp.

Her hair fell in tangled waves as he drove into her from behind. He talked dirty to her in Spanish, whispering the words into the back of her neck. Her fingers gripped the pillows, and she curled her spine, undulating her hips against each magnificent thrust.

"Camila." The sound of her name was a hoarse growl from a man losing control.

He gripped her wrists and bound both hands to the pillows. She was completely and utterly dominated by him. "I'm coming," she gasped, and came with a vengeance. Her entire body shook. The orgasm rocked her with the force of an earthquake.

She cried out like a wild woman, her fingernails biting into her palms as wave after wave of unbelievable pleasure swept through her and took control of her mind. Alejandro buried his face in the side of her neck and whispered her name in a hoarse, pained voice.

"Camila." He tensed, and then the same shudders rocked him too.

His fingers tightened around her wrists as he fought for control. But what they had experienced was too powerful to control. It couldn't be contained. He was as lost as she, tossed by the winds of ecstasy. With a final shudder, he collapsed on top of her. His full weight crushing her into the mattress. But she didn't want him to move. She could stay like this forever.

Alejandro kissed her ear and her cheek and then the corner of her mouth. She kissed him back with a soft moan of satisfaction. Rolling off her, he gathered her close and gently, carefully pushed her hair off her forehead.

"I must look like a mess," she whispered.

"You look beautiful. Like a woman who has been made love to."

He tilted her chin higher and placed a tender kiss on her lips. When he lifted his head, he gazed down into her eyes, almost as if searching for something.

"*Te amo*, Xochitl."

Her heart melted. She loved when he called her by her first name.

"*Te he amado toda mi vida*," he said. *I have loved you all my life.*

Happy tears filled her eyes. "*Yo también. Te he amado toda mi vida.*"

17

Camila came out of the bathroom dressed in a white sleeveless top and white panties. Alejandro was lying on the bed and let his eyes trail down her luscious body, a smile affixed to his face.

She stopped and rested her hands on her hips. "Why are you smiling?"

Sitting up against the pillows, he folded his arms behind his head. "I am remembering the first time I saw you in a bathing suit back in Jalisco, and we went swimming in the river. You wore a white suit. You were fifteen."

She laughed softly. "Oh yeah, I worked up the courage to wear a suit around you boys. Before that, I always wore old shorts and a tank top. Did you like what you saw?"

"*Por supuesto,*" Alejandro said adamantly.

Her cheeks turned a rosy hue at his vehemence. "Do you know what I remember? You didn't say anything. You stared at me, and I was so self-conscious those first few minutes."

"I didn't mean to make you self-conscious, but I couldn't talk. I had swallowed my tongue." He remembered the day like it was yesterday. He, Emilio, and her had gone down to the river to cool off. When she removed her pants and pulled off her top, it was like his every fantasy had come true. His body reacted, and he had to dive into the water to cool off.

Camila padded over and straddled him on the bed. She flattened her palm against the silky hairs on his bare chest. "Those were good times," she whispered.

"Yes."

They had been young, with no clue of the changes that would rock their lives as they became older.

"I looked forward to those summers," Alejandro said.

"Me too." Then she lowered her eyes, as if hiding something.

"*¿Qué pasa*, hmm?" He titled up her chin with his middle finger, forcing her to look at him again.

She swallowed deeply. "There's something I have to tell you, about me and Emilio."

His stomach knotted. He didn't want to talk about Emilio.

"Tell me," he said, though he worried what she was about to say would crack the newly established peace between them.

Camila breathed out slowly through her mouth. "Things weren't great between Emilio and I before he died."

Granted, he hadn't been as close with his old friend as when they were younger, but this was news to him. "What do you mean?"

She bent her head again. "We were having problems. We hadn't gotten along for a long time. He was seeing someone else."

"Are you sure?" Emilio had been cheating on Camila? His brain couldn't compute behavior so outrageous.

She nodded. "I confronted him, and he admitted it."

"How long had—" The question broke off in disbelief.

She shrugged. "He said only a few months, but I believe the affair went on much longer."

"Did you know the woman?"

"Yes. She was someone he worked with in the cash room at the casino."

Alejandro ran a hand over his head in disbelief. "Camila, I'm sorry. I am in shock. What you're saying does not sound like Emilio. I don't understand why he would do that."

Fury emerged beneath the shock. How dare he cheat on her? How dare he hurt her in that way?

"It wasn't his fault."

"I know you're not blaming yourself."

"It was my fault, Alejandro—"

"No!" He sat up, enraged she blamed herself for Emilio's actions. "There is no excuse for cheating."

She fell quiet, tucking her dark hair behind her ear. "You don't understand," she said in a low voice.

"What don't I understand? You were married. You made vows to each other."

She rolled off him and onto the floor. Wrapping her arms around herself, she faced away from him, as if gathering strength to speak.

When she finally faced him again, he recognized a combination of grief and guilt in her expression. "I was wrong to accept his proposal when I didn't love him the way I should have, and I'm the reason he's dead."

Alejandro flung his legs over the side of the bed. "I don't know why you're saying this, but unless you were driving the truck that hit him when he ran through the stop sign, you had nothing to do with his death."

"He wouldn't have been in the car if not for *me*. We fought that night. We argued about his cheating."

"How is the argument your fault?" Alejandro demanded.

"Listen!" she pleaded. "H-he said he wouldn't have been involved with the other woman if I were a better wife. An honest wife. If—if he didn't know about my feelings for you. He called me a cheater, in my heart."

Alejandro couldn't believe what he was hearing.

"He guessed my feelings for you and was jealous. Jealous of you and what I felt for you. He said he saw it every time you came to visit. The big stud. I think he resented the fact that you were bigger than him and stronger. He complained about when you were kids and the other kids messed with him, and you had to jump in."

Alejandro was bigger and stronger than most of the other children in their neighborhood. When they bullied Emilio, he stepped in. After a while, no one messed with him because he had his own personal security.

"I protected him because he was my friend."

"I know, and I believe at the time he appreciated your help. But later, as we grew older, those memories became embarrassing instances of his weakness and inability to defend himself."

Alejandro ran a hand over his head again. "*Jesús Cristo*, what you're telling me..."

"I know. It's hard to accept. Emilio wasn't the same person we knew as children. He changed, and the truth is, I wanted to be free of him. We used to be friends, but at some point in the marriage, I lost my friend, and then I lost him permanently in the worst possible way. For good."

Alejandro extended a hand to her, and she took it. "You should not blame yourself for what happened to Emilio. Whatever he felt about me, was his problem. I did not know you had feelings for me, Camila. Had I known..." Then a day, long ago, came back to him, and disappointment tightened his chest. "The summer you turned sixteen, I told Emilio about my feelings for you."

Her eyes widened. "You did?"

He nodded. "I was worried about telling you—worried my confession would affect our relationship. I confided in him, and he said he would talk to you for me. Then the next thing I know, you were a couple. He told me, with regret, that when he spoke to you, you expressed your feelings for him."

She stepped back, shock on her face. "Wait, I remember when he came to me, but he said he had feelings for me, and you had encouraged him to tell me about his feelings."

Alejandro muttered a curse. "That is not what happened."

Her eyes widened again, and she put a hand to her mouth. "He lied to keep us apart," she said softly.

Alejandro didn't want to believe what she was saying, but it was the only explanation that made sense. Emilio couldn't have misunderstood what he had said to him.

"Then you started dating," he said, the pain as fresh as ever.

"When we told you, you didn't react. You behaved as if you didn't care."

"What could I do except pretend I was happy for the two of you? His family had been good to me and my grand-mother. I remember times when we struggled, and they invited us into their home to eat. Emilio was like a brother to me, and as far as I was concerned, you had chosen the better man."

"*You* were the better man, and I thought you didn't want me the way I wanted you."

Alejandro's jaw tightened, and he pulled her close again. "No," he said, the word torn from between tight lips. "I wanted you. I have always wanted you."

She straddled his thighs and placed her hands on his shoulders. Neither of them spoke for a while, but anger, disappointment, and a maddening sense of betrayal rolled through him. For so long, he'd believed he had no right to touch this woman. A woman he had longed for, and who for years he had tried to exorcise from his thoughts with the bodies of other women. To no avail.

Casual sex, while quenching the thirst of his body, had always left him empty because none of the dozens of women he'd slept with had come close to giving him the satisfaction he achieved tonight with Camila.

To think, all this time, she could have been his. They could have been together, but his so-called friend, his so-called brother, had kept them apart.

"*Pinche cabrón,*" he muttered.

Camila stroked his bearded jaw. "I feel sorry for him. He must have been hurting and terribly insecure."

"I do not feel sorry for him," Alejandro said, barely able to suppress his rage.

"I've had time to think about the past in a way you haven't."

"You should have told me before what he said and what he did."

"I should have, but I didn't know how. Your relationship with him was always different from mine with you."

"Don't think about it anymore. It's in the past." Alejandro cupped her bottom. He would not allow his anger to shift to her. It should remain on Emilio where it belonged.

"Do you think he's the reason you went to prison?" she whispered. "What if he was the person who told the police what you did?"

"It's possible, but we will never know for sure."

He'd thought the same thing at one time because Camila and Emilio were the only people who knew what he'd done. No way his friend could have—would have—turned him in. At least, he hadn't wanted to believe that, and so he'd dismissed the idea and accepted his fate.

"I'm going downstairs to get some water. Do you want anything from the kitchen?" Camila asked.

"I'm fine. Thank you."

"Be right back." Camila kissed him briefly and left him in the bedroom with his thoughts.

Alejandro rested his elbows on his knees and recalled "the incident" that occurred when he was seventeen and changed the trajectory of his life. Losing Camila had made him restless, and he'd been looking for a reason to get into trouble. The local church was robbed by a gang who had been terrorizing the community for years, and Father Gonzalez—Emilio's father—said he was praying about it. Alejandro decided to do more and plotted to get the money and goods back. And he did, all by himself, anonymously returning what the gang hadn't spent or distributed among themselves.

Then he decided to teach the thugs a lesson. He waited until the house that served as the base for their operations was empty, and he planted homemade bombs, using Tang as an accelerant with hydrogen peroxide. Except the house wasn't empty like he thought. The gang's leader was asleep inside and died in the explosion.

At first, Alejandro had been horrified that he'd killed someone, but the town celebrated the gang leader's demise. Alejandro became a hero, but no one knew. He confided in Emilio and Camila. Within two weeks, he was arrested and thrown into prison. But for some reason, he was kept separate from the other inmates, and he soon learned why.

A top-secret U.S. government organization, Plan B, was recruiting internationally and learned about his situation. They offered a way out if he came to work for them. Otherwise, he'd be thrown into gen pop and would have to fend for himself against the gang's incarcerated members.

He joined Plan B.

He said goodbye to his grandmother, Emilio, and had an especially emotional conversation with Camila, who had already returned to the States. For more than two years, he disappeared as he was trained. His specialty became engineering and explosives. He learned how much explosives to use to bring down a building, where to plant them for the best structural collapse, how to make his own homemade devices, and much more—making him a lethal adversary who could cause major destruction.

Having to disappear for such a long period of time never upset him. Knowing Emilio and Camila were in a relationship made leaving easy. He threw himself into his training and didn't see his friends again until he was almost twenty.

Friends. He didn't have many of those, and trust didn't come easy, but that's what he'd thought of Camila and Emilio. He had no doubt Camila was genuine, but now he knew Emilio was a liar, a backstabber, and probably the traitor who'd turned him in to the police at seventeen.

That *hijo de puta* was lucky he was already dead because, if he was still alive, Alejandro would have killed him.

18

Riding in the passenger seat with Alejandro driving, Camila tried to put a name to the emotion that filled her.

Happiness.

The only way to describe her current state.

For the longest time, she had lived in a fog of regret and then guilt. Now, because of the conversation she and Alejandro had last night, the veil had lifted, and she was in a good place.

Earlier this morning, a police officer called and notified her that her house was clear to re-enter, and right on time. After visiting with the coroner, who'd agreed to meet them this morning, they had an afternoon flight to Tijuana and would arrive a little after seven in the evening. Now she could easily go into the house to collect her passport and clothes for the trip. She had already turned in her article, so she had the next few days free.

As for the prepaid phone Melissa bought for Doug, Camila's contact at the police department stated there was no phone logged in evidence. Alejandro and Camila agreed that if he was murdered as suspected, the killers took it. Which means they knew he had called Camila.

When they arrived at the one-story brick building, Alejandro drove around the landscape island in the middle of the lot to an empty parking space, and then they went inside. They had a thirty-minute wait seated in uncomfortable metal chairs in the hall before the medical examiner, Dr. Ray Stenner, arrived with a brisk walk.

"My apologies for keeping you waiting. Please, follow me." They were meeting in his office instead of the examination room.

"Thank you." Camila took the chair in front of his desk while Alejandro stood behind her with his shoulder resting on the bookcase, arms folded across his midsection.

Dr. Stenner was an older man with a long face and his dark hair mostly gray. He adjusted his white coat as he sat behind his desk. "Vicky told me about your concerns. I know you write for *The Pulse*. Is this regarding one of your articles? I remember the series you did—what was it—"Invisible Lives"? Heartbreaking but eye-opening stories about the homeless population."

"Thank you. I put a lot of time and effort into the stories. I thought it was important to humanize them. I learned a lot about their struggles, their dreams, their past lives, but also how we as a society treat them and how we can do better."

He nodded. "I agree. I admired your work. How can I help you with this project?"

She didn't correct him, suspecting he would be more forthcoming with information if he believed she was writing another piece for the magazine.

"I have a question about Doug Duvall. Vicky explained his death was ruled a suicide, but I don't think that's possible. The shot was in his right temple, which means he used his right hand—except Doug had an injury that kept him from lifting his arm all the way up. There's no way he could have put a gun to his own head—at least, not on the right side."

Dr. Stenner flipped open a folder on his desk. "I understand what you're saying, and Vicky explained all this to me when she left the message that you'd be following up. However, I'm sorry to tell you, I think you must have made a mistake. Could it have been his left arm?"

"No, I'm certain his right arm was damaged. As a matter-of-fact, he owned a little dog, and he always held her on his left side for that reason."

"Hmm." The doctor tapped his chin as he reviewed the file.

Camila looked at the paperwork but couldn't read the words upside down. She shot a glance at Alejandro, who was zeroed in on the doctor's bent head.

Dr. Stenner looked up. "I'm sorry, but given the trajectory of the bullet and the weapon found at the scene, the evidence supports suicide—unless you have evidence or information to suggest another party was involved in the shooting."

Camila's shoulders slumped. "I don't."

"Were his hands tested for gunshot residue?" Alejandro asked.

"Yes, they were, and there was gunshot residue on his right hand."

"You already have the results back?" He sounded surprised.

"Yes, we do."

Alejandro straightened. "Test results typically take a few days. I have only seen a fast turnaround for high-profile cases, and I would not call this a high-profile case."

Dr. Stenner shifted in his leather chair and steepled his fingers. "You're right, but since Mr. Duvall's sister was coming to pick up his body, we wanted to have the answers for her right away, so I personally put a rush on the testing."

"That was kind of you."

Dr. Stenner's smile looked strained. "I'm sorry, who are you again?"

"Alejandro Sanchez. I'm a friend of Camila, but I work for The Cordoba Agency—a security company—as a bodyguard and investigator."

"I see. Well, I assure you, the speed with which the test results are obtained is at the full discretion of the medical examiner, and in this case, I wanted to make sure we had those results for Ms. Duvall before she left. I know this isn't the answer you both wanted, but it appears Mr. Duvall committed suicide. If indeed his arm was bothering him, maybe the range of motion improved without your knowledge." He closed the folder.

Camila took his movement as a dismissal. "Thank you for your time, Dr. Stenner."

"I'm always happy to help. Keep up the good work on those articles."

Camila rose from the chair, and they exited his office.

Outside, she walked slowly toward the car. "Could I have been wrong? Maybe his arm did get better," she mused.

"I doubt it," Alejandro said.

"You doubt what the medical examiner said?"

"He wasn't telling the whole truth, and I trust you more than I trust him."

They climbed into the gray Honda, but Alejandro didn't start the car, his attention trained out the window.

"What's wrong?" Camila asked.

"There's something odd about the guy in the old Dodge over there."

She leaned forward to take a look past him, and sure enough, a man with straight, shoulder-length blond hair sat in a navy-blue two-door. The car was backed into its parking space, and the occupant was looking away from them in the direction of the traffic.

"Maybe he's meeting someone."

"Maybe. Or he's watching us. He was there when we arrived, and we spent at least thirty minutes waiting for the medical examiner. Then when we climbed into this car, he started his vehicle. Now he's just sitting there."

Camila instantly became nervous as she recalled the home invasion from the other night. Was he someone else sent to harm them? "What should we do?"

"Find out who he is, and why he's following us."

Alejandro started the car, but instead of driving out of the lot, he pulled into the middle of the pathway, blocking the man from getting out. "Be right back."

Camila watched him stroll toward the other car. At first, the stranger kept his eyes downcast, but finally he looked up, and Alejandro stopped in the middle of the lot. Even from this distance, she saw the tension in his body.

Why did he stop? she wondered as both men had a stare down.

Then the driver hit the gas.

"Jandro!" Camila screamed, almost breaking the seat belt and coming out of her seat.

Alejandro vaulted onto the hood and ran over the top of the vehicle—like someone running on a treadmill—and fell in a roll onto his side. The driver swung left to avoid hitting the Honda. He bumped over the parking island, the bottom of his car scraping the curb. He dropped back onto the asphalt and shot toward the exit, swiping a MINI Cooper and knocking off its side mirror in the process.

Alejandro shot to his feet and raced past her to chase the vehicle down the street.

"What the hell?" Camila whispered.

A woman was standing in the doorway of the coroner's building, staring after the commotion with her mouth hanging open.

Camila unhooked her seatbelt and scrambled into the driver's seat. She started the car and drove in the direction Alejandro had gone. She had just turned out of the lot when he came jogging toward her.

"Are you okay?" a man in a parked car called out.

Alejandro waved at him. "I'm fine." He walked up to the driver's side, barely winded.

Camila scooted over so he could climb in. "Are we going after him?"

He shook his head and shifted the car into gear. "He's long gone."

"Did you get the license plate? I have a friend at the DMV. We could find out who he was."

He shook his head, frustration evident in the tightening of his jawline. "He had a ghost plate on the car."

"A ghost plate?" Camila had never heard the expression before.

"That means the plate was partially hidden. Looks like he used plastic, so I only saw the first two numbers."

"Darn," Camila whispered. "Are you okay? You're not hurt?" She placed a hand on his arm.

"I'm fine." He gripped the steering wheel.

"I thought for sure he was going to hit you. How did you do that?"

He shot her a look, the right corner of his mouth lifting higher into that roguish smile she was familiar with. "Years of practice."

Camila arched an eyebrow. "One of these days, you're going to tell me what you did before you became a bodyguard."

"One of these days," he agreed. "Until then, we need to go to your house and pack for our trip. From here on out, we need to be extra careful. Whoever is after you—or us—was trying to put us under surveillance. They're not going to give up trying to stop us from uncovering what's going on." His expression turned grim again.

"Do you think it was Reyes?"

"Yes, and when we get back from Tijuana, we need to figure out how to deal with him."

Their eyes met, and Camila gulped. Going up against Javier Reyes would be no easy task. If only half the rumors about him were true, he'd be a formidable opponent. The only reason fear didn't engulf her was because Alejandro was by her side.

19

"This is a mess!" Dr. David Shapiro ran shaky fingers through his hair.

From behind his desk, Javier Reyes critically observed his longtime friend as he paced Javier's office atop the Celestial Palace Hotel & Casino. With his graying black hair, David would be considered distinguished-looking if he didn't have such a weak chin and let himself go as he grew older. His lean, muscular frame was long gone and replaced by soft arms and a soft middle. Meanwhile, Javier exercised regularly with a trainer, spent three hundred dollars on his biweekly hair trim, and colored his hair to maintain a polished appearance.

"It's not a mess. You told me to take care of the problem, and I took care of it."

"You call taking care of it leaving his body behind the market? Your men should have moved him somewhere else."

"What difference does it make? He's dead. When he came to you demanding money in exchange for keeping his mouth shut about what he had discovered, you asked for my help. I sent my men after him. The situation has been handled, and his body will be shipped to his sister in California. Very soon, this will all be behind you."

"This isn't just my problem. He has pictures of the two of us."

"Those pictures are more damning for you than they are for me. Everybody already knows I'm a piece of shit. Besides, they're not incriminating photos." Javier was getting bored with the conversation. He walked over to the bar. "Can I fix you a drink?"

David looked at him as if he was crazy. "It's ten o'clock in the morning."

"Your point?"

David rolled his eyes skyward. "No, thank you, I don't want a drink. I want that nosy reporter and her boyfriend to go away."

"In due time. Dr. Stenner should be able to convince them Doug died of suicide. Once that's complete, I don't anticipate they'll be a problem anymore."

"You need to keep an eye on her. If she goes digging—"

"Digging for what? She doesn't know anything." Javier poured himself a cognac.

"You're awfully confident."

"Why shouldn't I be? We've made a lot of money the past seven years."

"You more than me," David mumbled, dropping his gaze.

"Because I'm the one with the capital, David—or did you forget? I bailed you out when your clinic was going under, remember? I infused it with cash and offered you the opportunity to expand by diversifying."

"Diversifying is what you call what we do?"

"What would you call offering transplant services? If you no longer want to be involved, say the word, and—"

"I didn't say that. I'm just nervous."

"You're always nervous, and I always take care of our problems—don't I?"

His friend let out a deep breath. "Yes, you do."

"My job is to take care of the problems, and your job is to take care of the medical aspects of our business."

David had been the one who found surgeons willing to do the transplants off the books for a cut.

"And of course keep your wife happy," Javier continued. "How is the lovely Kathleen these days?"

"Fine. She's in New York, visiting her mother." He inhaled deeply and let the air out his mouth, something he did often to calm his nerves.

He went through the calming exercise several more times while Javier sipped his morning cognac, enjoying the burn as the liquid slid down his throat.

"You'll let me know what happens?" David asked.

"Of course. Stop worrying. Everything will be fine."

David nodded, though he looked doubtful, and left Javier alone in the office. Swirling the reddish-brown liquid in his glass, he walked over to one of the large windows.

This used to be his father's corner office, and now it belonged to him. From here, he had a good view of the strip, including the other property he was in the midst of renovating, the Pampered Princess—a princess-themed hotel and casino. When the contractors completed the work, it would be a one of a kind experience catering to female clientele.

There would be a women-only club offering dancing and entertainment, a world-class spa with a beauty bar and salon, as well as wellness programs, yoga studios, and meditation classes designed for women. Other parts of the casino would be limited to female guests, including one of the pools, where they could relax and enjoy the luxurious cabanas—again, without the unwanted attention of men.

He'd gotten the idea for the concept when Kathleen mentioned how much she enjoyed the women-only train compartments in Japan and Dubai. He realized there was a market for that kind of thing, even if he thought it was utterly ridiculous. His father might not have thought he was very smart, but he'd proven to be brilliant in business, growing their holdings by ten percent since taking control a year ago by implementing innovative ideas.

And to think, his father had wanted his second in command to take control of the company because he didn't believe in Javier—his own flesh and blood. Had called him morally bankrupt and his "mother's son" as a way to insult him and insinuate he didn't have the brains needed to take control of the Reyes empire.

Well, he had proven him wrong, and now everyone knew what he was capable of.

His private line rang, and he picked up on the second ring, already knowing who was calling because he'd been waiting for the call.

"Yes?"

"It's me."

He placed his cognac on the desk and sat down, crossing his legs. "How did the meeting go?"

"I think I convinced them that it was a suicide," Dr. Stenner replied.

"You *think*? You better have convinced them." He paid handsomely for absolutes. Not maybes.

He was still upset his man had been discovered in the parking lot of Dr. Stenner's building. Fortunately, he escaped, but Javier hated he had been noticed in the first place, a development he'd purposely kept from David because he was already acting like a nervous ninny. He'd wanted his man to keep tabs on the couple—find out where they were staying and what their next moves would be.

"I did convince them, but I believe the man could be a problem. He seemed... skeptical."

Alejandro Sanchez.

Javier flipped open the file on his desk and looked at the photo of the man inside who had killed two of his men. He was an agent for The Cordoba Agency, a company based out of Georgia with an excellent reputation, but there was an aura of mystery surrounding them. His people were still doing research, but so far he was intrigued.

"Is that all?" Javier asked.

"Er, I'm just wondering, was this visit because she was writing another article? It wasn't clear."

Javier ignored the question. "I'll be in touch if I need anything else." He hung up.

He picked up his cognac again and took a sip. Pushing to his feet, he returned to the window. Despite his dismissive attitude toward David, he had concerns. He didn't know what Doug had told Camila, but she didn't seem to know much. If she and Mr. Sanchez discovered what was going on at the clinic, then he'd have a serious problem.

The idea of taking organs from the homeless had come from an unexpected place. His beloved mother.

After purchasing a kidney for her on the black market in Eastern Europe, she had lived for almost ten more years before he lost her to a heart attack. His father had been fine with the purchase of the kidney, but he didn't like the idea of Javier going into business supplying kidneys and other organs to people who could afford to buy them.

Selfish prick.

Why should people go without when willing donors existed? Why were people allowed to sell plasma, bone marrow, and eggs, but there was a prejudice against selling a kidney or part of a liver? At the time, Javier saw the opportunity to expand his finances beyond the paltry allowance his father gave him.

He did his research. He learned that an estimated seventeen people in the United States died every day waiting for an organ. There weren't enough to go around, but there were individuals willing to alleviate the shortage if they were compensated.

And so, he became part of the billion-dollar illegal organ selling trade. He started small with kidneys, using patients who came to the clinic, thanks to his good friend, David Shapiro. They'd paid them for their body parts—a thousand, two thousand dollars—while they made at least one hundred thousand during the sale. An incredible markup!

With such a return and the demand so great, they needed more inventory. The defining moment came when they needed a pancreas for an oil heiress in Texas. No one can live without a pancreas. Using the organs of the homeless could be hit or miss, but they'd been fortunate and taken the pancreas of a young homeless woman—someone who hadn't been on the streets very long, so she was very healthy.

The heiress had paid $400,000 for the pancreas, and the young woman—well, she ended up in a crematorium's furnace, her disappearance buried under layers of fake paperwork and bribes.

During the seven years since they had started, they expanded to Tijuana. Unbeknownst to David, Javier had also expanded to the Philippines, India, and Eastern Europe—all locations where he could receive a steady supply of organs from willing—or unwilling donors.

The buyers didn't know where the organs came from. They didn't care to know. They simply wanted to make their payment and go about their business, absolved of guilt. They weren't all rich either, but they were all desperate. Buyers had taken out second mortgages, drawn from their retirement accounts, sold family heirlooms—all to purchase something more valuable. Life.

His favorite was when there was a bidding war. That's when he netted the highest sales.

There were people who wouldn't understand what he was doing. It was easy to be dismissive until your own survival, or the survival of a family member, hung in the balance, desperation influencing what previously would have seemed to be an unthinkable choice.

Yes, there was plenty of money to be made. The ROI was extraordinary. But more importantly, he was providing a service. He was saving lives—most of the time. He was altruistic. A goddamn humanitarian.

Javier took another sip of his drink, chuckling to himself. He liked describing himself in those terms, and he liked making money. Lots of fucking money.

Hopefully, Ms. Hughes and Mr. Sanchez were going to mind their own business and move on. If not, he would make sure to solve that pesky little problem for good.

20

C amila hadn't been to Mexico in several years, but when she walked out of the terminal with Alejandro, the familiar sights and sounds of her mother's home country washed over her like an old friend.

Because of her appearance, people who didn't know her only saw a Black woman, but identifying only as Black meant ignoring half her DNA. The part that recognized the scent of warm tortillas and roasted chilies from the food stands nearby, which transported her to her childhood and working in the kitchen with her mommy and her *abuela*.

The bustling traffic, lively conversations in Spanish, and the distant sound of music put a smile on her face. Her heart swelled with a mixture of nostalgia and pride, confirming she had stayed away too long.

At the sound of a honking horn, Alejandro tapped her shoulder. He wore his cowboy hat and sunglasses. "There he is," he said, angling his chin in the direction of a taxicab.

The man who descended didn't look at all the way she had expected. She assumed he'd be Mexican. Instead, he looked like a walking ad for the California beach life. He was the same height as Alejandro with a similar build and handsome, with blond hair and stubble on his jaw that was a couple of shades darker. The grim set to his face softened as he approached.

"Good to see you, Sanchez," he said to Alejandro.

"Likewise." Both men shook hands and clapped each other on the back. "Buck, this is Camila Hughes. Camila, meet Buck Swanson, an old friend."

"Nice to meet you." Camila extended her hand, and his big palm swallowed hers in a firm handshake.

"The pleasure is all mine." He took their bags and started toward his white cab with *Taxi Libre* written in bright orange on the side. "First time in Tijuana, Camila?" he asked over his shoulder.

"Yes, if you can believe that," she replied.

"Sanchez, you've been here before, haven't you?"

"Once. For work."

Buck popped the trunk and placed their bags inside. "I'll tell you all the good places to eat."

"How long have you lived here?" Camila asked.

"Only two weeks, but I've visited before. Still haven't decided if I'll stay for good. Maybe I will if the money works out."

"Where are you from originally?" Camila asked.

"Texas. A little town called Dripping Springs. Ever heard of it?"

"No," she admitted.

"No one has," he said with a laugh. "It's near Austin."

They climbed into the taxi, Alejandro in the back seat and Camila in the passenger seat. On the way to their destination, they passed by beautiful murals on the walls of buildings, designed with bright colors depicting local history and social themes. The roads were filled with vehicles, and vendors sold street food and fresh fruit on the sidewalks. There was definitely an energy to the place as locals and visitors mingled in the early evening.

There were lots of billboards promoting medical tourism, offering quality healthcare at affordable prices for a variety of procedures such as dental care and cosmetic surgery. The most popular areas to have work done were Zona Río, Playas de Tijuana, and Zona Centro. Each offered a different setting. Zona Río, for example, was a commercial district with modern infrastructure and upscale shops. Playas de Tijuana, on the other hand, offered a more relaxing experience near the ocean.

Buck pulled up to a light-blue, nondescript building with small restaurants and cafes all around. He waited in the small lobby while they checked in and went upstairs.

Their room was small but neat. Nothing fancy, but they had a view of the street below and a small iron balcony with two metal chairs and a metal table.

Camila rested her hands on her hips as she looked around. "One bed?" She arched an eyebrow. "What did you have in mind?"

Alejandro chuckled and walked over to where she stood. "What do you think I have in mind?" he whispered against her neck.

A thrill rippled through her, and she slipped her arms around his waist and gazed up at him.

"A little more of what we did last night?" she suggested.

"You want more, eh?"

"A little bit," she admitted.

"That can be arranged," he said.

His kiss was warm, his lips tugging on hers and causing her body to tingle all over. Was this real life? Was she really allowed to touch and kiss him at will?

She ground her hips against his, and he pulled back regretfully. "Buck is waiting downstairs. We're going to dinner with him."

Camila watched him closely. "Is he really a taxi driver?"

"Why do you ask?"

Interesting. He didn't answer the question—not that answering would help. The problem with Alejandro was, she couldn't tell when he was lying. She could tell when he was upset, but he had a poker face when it came to telling untruths.

"He doesn't look like a cab driver," she said, picking up her purse from where she'd placed it on the bed.

"What does a cab driver look like?" he asked, amusement in his eyes.

"Not him, for sure. He looks like a bodyguard, like you."

"Less chance of people trying to take advantage of him, I suppose. Come on," he said.

Alejandro took her hand, which felt like the most natural move in the world. They met Buck downstairs and walked across the street to a bar, where the enticing scent of roasting meat and other delicacies filled their nostrils as they entered.

They sat at a table, Alejandro and Camila next to each other, with Buck across from them. The waitress placed a bowl of red salsa and a bowl of green salsa on the table with chips. She brought both men Tecate beers and coconut water for Camila. With their beverages in front of them, Buck gave an update while they waited for the food to arrive.

"You have an appointment with Dr. Lima at eleven, but you'll actually meet with Rosa. She's a doctor's assistant at the clinic and is the reason you were able to get squeezed in on such short notice. I told her you were journalists who want to expose the illegal trafficking of organs. When you arrive, make sure you mention her name as the person who referred you."

"How far are we from the clinic?" Alejandro asked, taking a drag on his bottle.

"Only a few miles. Because it's on the outskirts of the city, if you drive a little ways beyond the clinic, you'll hit dirt roads and houses farther apart."

Dr. Shapiro's clinic was called Oasis de Vida. Clinics on the edge of town were smaller and performed niche services such as stem cell therapy and bariatric surgery. According to their website, Oasis de Vida offered the same therapy in Tijuana as he did in Las Vegas, but she and Alejandro were certain he had chosen the area because it was less policed than the established medical zones. Which meant it was easier for him to get away with his illegal activity, assuming they were correct.

Buck leaned closer. "Listen, if you're right, this thing is bigger than a clinic. For a business like this to flourish, there has to be other people in the network."

"I thought about that. Medical examiner, police officers, crematoriums," Alejandro said.

"Exactly."

Camila shivered. She hadn't considered the other people necessary to make the illegal buying and selling of organs into a successful enterprise.

"I appreciate you finding her and setting the appointment for us," Alejandro said.

"Not a problem. I've made a few friends and connections since I've been here. Oh, before I forget, here are the keys to my car. It's a white Honda HR-V parked in the lot behind the hotel."

Alejandro took the keys. "Thank you."

"For the rest of the night, relax, eat some good food, and then go to your appointment in the morning."

"I like that plan." Alejandro tapped his bottle to Buck's and took another swig of his beer.

Their food arrived shortly thereafter, and for the rest of the night, their conversation remained lighthearted, with Buck sharing tales of his escapades as a young boy growing up in the small Texas town. He was clearly a handful for his parents.

They told him stories about the town in Jalisco where they

met. Before long, a couple of hours had passed, and it was time for them to go their separate ways.

Outside the restaurant, Buck and Alejandro shook hands. "Good luck."

"You're certain she'll be there?" Alejandro asked.

"Positive," Buck said with a nod.

"*Gracias, güey.*"

Buck walked away, and they went up to the room.

Alejandro took a shower first and Camila went in after him. When she came out of the bathroom, she found him on the balcony, wearing only his jeans and his sunglasses. No shirt or shoes and smoking a cigar.

She wrapped her arms around his neck from behind. "Are you coming to bed anytime soon?"

"In a little bit."

He offered her a smoke, and she took the cigar, taking several puffs before handing it back to him.

She put her back to the iron railing and looked down at the street below, where cars cruised by and people idled near the doorways of the retail establishments, chatting with friends.

"If Señora Carrizosa saw you smoking with me, she would say I'm a bad influence," Alejandro said.

Her eyes returned to him. "She wouldn't be wrong. You're the reason I started smoking cigars." She noted the thoughtful expression on his face. "What are you thinking about?"

He slowly removed his sunglasses and placed them on the table. "Tomorrow. I don't think you should come."

Camila sighed heavily. "We had this conversation on the plane. I'm coming. I want to come."

"This could get dangerous."

"You think I don't know that? It's already dangerous, but we can't stop now."

"I don't plan to stop, but I think you should stay at the hotel while I—"

"No. I didn't get on a six-hour flight and come all the way down here to sit in the hotel room while you go check out the facility. Four eyes are better than two, and we're a team now."

He watched her in silence.

"Jandro, we're here to gather information, but more importantly, I want to stop Dr. Shapiro and Javier Reyes. Whatever we learn tomorrow could help shut down their operation, and I want to be a part of making that happen. Maybe I'm being selfish, but I'm pissed off they killed my friend and might get away with his murder. I'm pissed off they've hurt other people and might get away with it. I want to stop them."

"Reyes already tried to take you out once. If we destroy his business, he is not going to be happy."

Watching the white smoke snake its way upward into the night, Camila knew he was right, but if they were correct about what he was doing, she wanted to be a part of stopping him "Whatever happens, it's worth the risk," she said.

Alejandro leaned forward. "Tomorrow, if the situation goes south, you do exactly what I say. *¿Comprendes?*"

"*Sí, está bien.*"

"This time, you will follow my lead?"

"Yes, I promise."

"Because I don't want anything to happen to you." He spoke with feeling and a fierceness that gave her comfort.

"I'll be fine, and I promise to do whatever you tell me. Besides, I know whatever happens, I'm safe with you."

Alejandro sat back. Their conversation had allayed his concerns. For now.

21

"Where do you want to go for breakfast?" Camila asked, looking over her shoulder at Alejandro as he came out of the bathroom.

Last night they'd climbed into bed and fallen asleep without making love. Looking at her now, his body stirred with desire, and the last thing on his mind was food. With the morning light streaming in through the sheer white curtains, he paused in awe of her beauty.

Her long, chocolate mane tumbled down her back like a silken waterfall. The rich tresses moved with her as she tied the right shoulder strap of her mustard-yellow sundress.

"Anywhere is fine with me." He came up behind her and swept her hair over one shoulder to plant a kiss on her exposed neck.

Now he had the right to touch her, that's all he wanted to do. He had only been living as half a person before. This newfound intimacy with Camila made him feel whole.

He slid his arms around her waist, and she leaned back, pressing her soft bottom into his hardening shaft.

"What time is our appointment?" She reached back and caressed his bearded jaw.

"He said eleven, which means we have plenty of time."

Alejandro cupped her breasts and squeezed their fullness in his hands, listening to her soft moans of pleasure. He turned her around and kissed her, starting slowly at first by nibbling gently at her lips. But her mouth was like candy—sweet and addictive. He deepened the kiss, tangling his tongue with hers as he slid his hands lower to cup her soft ass.

He walked her backward and pushed her onto the bed, coming down on top of her and dragging his mouth down her neck to where the fabric covered her breasts. Damn, she always smelled so good, like pineapple and honey.

He pulled down the top and pushed her hardened nipples above the neckline. She gasped and trembled as he licked her dark areola and teased her nipples with the edge of his teeth. She moaned again and writhed her core against his hardened length.

Her hands became busy undoing the button on his jeans and then lowering the zipper, but Alejandro wasn't ready for the finale yet. He stood on the side of the bed, aroused by the delectable image she presented with her hemline pushed halfway up her partially open legs and her lovely breasts spilling over the top of her dress.

He pulled aside her panties and dropped to his knees so he could eat her properly. With every stroke of his tongue, she undulated her hips and scraped her fingernails in the sheets. She tasted so sweet, so succulent, he could stay there all day with his face between her thighs and listen to her half moan and half cry as he drove her insane.

She was so wet and ready, he was anxious to feel the tight clasp of her sex around him and pushed to his feet. Gripping her bottom with possessive hands, he lifted her from the bed and sat down with her straddling his lap.

He was extremely hard, almost afraid he'd come before he could slide inside her. He rolled backward and released himself, watching with bated breath as she dipped her head toward his pelvis with a naughty smile. At first contact, his body jerked. She licked his erection from the bottom to the top, then closed her full lips over the tip and sucked, humming in the back of her throat.

Watching her mouth stretched full of him was a wonderfully erotic sight he couldn't tear his eyes away from. She teased him for a bit longer before she climbed on top of him and slid down one tantalizing inch at a time.

Her mouth had been incredible, but having her body clasp his was mind-blowing. She was tight and sopping wet. He let her control the depth of penetration but held her hips to control the pace. They moved in perfect synchronous motion as she rode him. He shifted his hands higher to fondle her breasts and watched with satisfaction at the passion displayed on her face.

She whimpered, placing her hands on his bare chest, her pelvis moving atop his in a circular motion. He shuddered as her fingernails scraped his hard nipples. Thrusting faster, he held her bound to him with one hand on her hip.

At the same time her orgasmic contractions started, her lips parted on a soft cry. He watched with fascination as she rode out the storm, breasts jostling as she bounced up and down, head thrown back and eyes closed.

"Yes, yes," she gasped.

Only as she was coming down off her high did he allow himself to let go. He came with an animalistic groan, his fingers tightening for a millisecond on her hip. She collapsed on top of him as waves of pleasure crashed into his body and had him thrusting his hips in a frantic attempt to wring every bit of ecstasy he could from the moment.

Their mouths collided in a heated rush. Wild and unrestrained as he ground his pelvis into hers. Cupping her face, he tangled his fingers in her silky brown hair. Strands fell across his cheek and onto the mattress. Hungrily, they devoured each other, their breaths mingling in quick, uneven bursts. The imperfect rawness of the kiss left him breathless and panting, as if he'd run full speed through an obstacle course.

When it was over, they both lay spent, their bodies still intimately joined.

Camila trailed her fingers through the silky hairs on his chest. "That was…"

"*Increíble*," he supplied.

He felt rather than saw her smile.

"*Sí, increíble*," she agreed.

Moments later, Camila slipped off Alejandro and stood beside the bed.

He pushed onto his elbows. "You're so sexy," he whispered.

She blushed, her cheeks turning rosy as she pulled up her top to cover the spill of her breasts. "So are you, Mr. Sanchez. I'm going to clean up."

She went into the bathroom, and he fell back onto the mattress. Never in a million years had he imagined having this type of connection with Camila. He tried not to be resentful, but the truth was, if Emilio hadn't lied to them both, they could have been sharing many more moments like this. They would probably be married, with a couple of kids.

Kids. A family.

What kind of father would he be? He hoped a good one, but he already knew Camila would be a wonderful mother. Her compassionate nature, care for the homeless, and dogged pursuit of the truth were a good indication.

He stood and tucked his penis into his pants. Inside the bathroom, Camila was at the sink using a washcloth to clean herself up. When he entered, she smiled at him in the mirror.

Alejandro braced his hands on either side of her and locked eyes in the mirror.

"Why are you looking at me like that?" she asked, with a faint smile.

"Why didn't you and Emilio have any kids?"

"Oh." She seemed taken aback by the question.

"Too personal?"

"No, I want us to be able to talk about anything. I didn't expect the question, that's all." She placed the washcloth on the counter. "He wanted to, but I kept putting it off."

"Why?"

She sighed. "In the beginning, we were both young and trying to figure out life together as a married couple. I didn't want to put a baby in the mix right away, but then as time went on, I realized I didn't want to have a baby... with him."

"Because you weren't sure you were going to stay together."

"Yes," she admitted.

Alejandro kissed her shoulder and then her neck. "You want to have children?" He kept his eyes on her in the mirror.

"Yes."

His arm snaked out and cinched around her waist to hold her close. "Would you have a baby with me?"

She covered his tattooed arm with her hands. "I would have lots of babies with you. How many do you want?"

Those had to be the sexiest words a woman had ever said to him. Alejandro felt himself harden again, and he poked his erection against her bottom.

"Three? Four?" he whispered huskily against the side of her neck as he lifted her dress to her waist.

Her breath hitched. "Not a problem."

He removed his thick shaft and pushed her legs wider with a swipe of his foot. Excitement flashed in her eyes.

Then he bent her over the sink, guided his body into hers, and fucked her again.

22

A lejandro and Camila ate a leisurely breakfast at one of the restaurants down the street and went with a typical Mexican meal. He ordered *chilaquiles* with eggs and a side of yogurt and fruit. Camila chose *huevos rancheros*. They both opted for freshly squeezed orange juice. After the meal, they went to the parking lot and found Buck's car.

Camila had been right about Buck. He was not just a taxi driver trying to decide if he wanted to live permanently in Tijuana. A former Navy SEAL, he was a member of the CIA's special missions team called the Omega Team. They specialized in sabotage, kidnapping, hostage rescue, and counterterrorism. Alejandro didn't know what his top-secret mission was in Tijuana, but he did know driving a taxi was simply a cover.

He opened the door and let Camila climb into the passenger seat, but the little minx brushed the front of his pants before she sat down, a mischievous smile on her face as she settled inside.

"You're in trouble when we get back to the hotel," he warned.

"Maybe you'll be the one in trouble," she said with a saucy grin.

He pinched her hip, and she slapped away his hand with a laugh.

The drive to Oasis de Vida didn't take long because the facility, as Buck had said, was only a few miles away. They were lucky enough to find parking on the street and eased into a slot about a block from the clinic in front of a multi-story office building. There wasn't a lot of foot traffic, but the clinic was nestled in a spot close to a number of businesses—a Peugeot and Honda car dealership side by side, a car wash, and a few small restaurants. Silver and modern, the place looked more like a sculpture than a medical clinic.

Hand in hand, Alejandro and Camila walked inside and up to the reception desk.

Alejandro lapsed into Spanish with the woman behind the counter. "Good morning. My name is Alejandro Sanchez, and I have an appointment with Dr. Lima. Rosa referred us."

The young woman checked the computer in front of her. "Yes, I see your appointment." She handed him a clipboard with a pen and several forms. "Please fill these out and bring them back when you're finished. I'll need to see your I.D. How will you be paying for the visit?"

"Out of pocket." He handed over his card and I.D.

He and Camila sat in the lobby with the rest of the potential patients. He did the bare minimum filling out the sheets. There weren't any questions setting off alarm bells, not that he was surprised. They were much too smart to bring undue attention to their illegal operation. On the form, Alejandro entered a knee injury as the reason he needed oxygen therapy and then handed in the paperwork.

Beside him, Camila bounced her left knee.

He placed a hand on her thigh, and she stopped. "Nervous?"

"A little. My stomach is in knots. I hope she's here and is willing to talk."

"So do I."

Less than ten minutes later, one of the doors leading into the waiting room opened, and a woman in her thirties wearing blue scrubs came out with a clipboard pressed to her chest.

"Alejandro Sanchez."

He and Camila rose from their chairs. "Hello, Rosa. Good to see you." He figured since she had been the one to allegedly refer them, they had to pretend to be friends.

"Good to see you too. Follow me, please." She shot a pleasant smile in their direction. If she was nervous, she was a great actress because he couldn't tell.

Instead of going through the usual motions of getting weighed and checking his blood pressure, Rosa took them immediately to one of the examination rooms. When they closed the door, she pressed her back against it and let out a sigh of relief.

"Hi." She swallowed.

"Are you okay?" Camila asked, placing a comforting hand on her arm.

"I am, but my heart is beating faster than usual."

"Take your time. We're not in a rush," Alejandro said.

She swallowed hard. "I don't have much time. If I take too long, one of the other staff members will know something is wrong," Rosa whispered. When she spoke again, her voice shook. "This job is not what I expected. I didn't sign up to—to be a criminal. I thought this was a legitimate healthcare facility, like the one I worked in before. At first, I didn't understand what was happening, but then I realized... *they're buying and selling organs here.*"

"How do you know?" Camila asked.

"I was here only two months when I noticed we don't have many patients for oxygen therapy. Two, maybe three in a whole day. We don't advertise our services, either. I also noticed there were parts of the clinic we weren't allowed to enter."

"'We' who?" Alejandro asked.

"Staff," she answered. "Upstairs, there's a separate operation, basically a separate business. You need a keycard to enter, and they have their own reception area. I only know this because I had to deliver files up there one day. Afterward, I started paying closer attention to what was happening around me. Patients were coming in through the back, which is why it took awhile for me to figure out what was happening. Chauffeurs pick them up—probably at the airport or from their hotel —and bring them here in vehicles with tinted windows."

"Who are these people?" Camila asked.

Rosa paused for a moment, listening at the door. The voices of two women talking and laughing could be heard going down the hall. After they passed, she continued. "I've done some digging on my own, and they come mostly from North America —Mexico, Canada, the United States. To a lesser degree, there are patients from Latin America."

She dug in her pocket and lifted out a jump drive. "A few weeks ago, I downloaded some files. I was going to the authorities, but then I got scared. What if they don't believe me? What if they're working with the clinic? I wish I weren't so afraid." Her lips quivered as they pressed into a thin pale line.

"It's understandable. The police are often bribed in organ trafficking operations. They turn a blind eye to what's happening right under their noses," Alejandro said.

"Here, take it. Buck said you're journalists, and you can be trusted." Her hands shook as she handed over the evidence to Camila. "You'll see most of the organs harvested are kidneys. But there are pancreases and hearts on the list. Donors can't live without those organs."

Alejandro and Camila exchanged a look. Silence filled the room as the horror of what she was suggesting sank in.

Camila slipped the device into the pocket of her dress. "We'll expose them and make sure the right people receive this information."

"Do you know where they're getting the organ donors from?" Alejandro asked.

"Locals, but refugees and migrants mostly, from what I can tell. They also come through the back. The organs have to be implanted in the recipient within thirty-six hours, which means all this has to happen quickly. Tests are run for compatibility and to make sure the organs are in good condition. Then the patient is contacted. They either have to arrive before the organ is removed or shortly thereafter, or it can't be implanted. One of the men who brings the donors, he's called The Transporter. I don't know his real name, but I've seen him more than any other driver. He's a big man. Anglo with black hair. Very pale. He always dresses in a white button-down shirt and slacks—as if he has a nice corporate job behind a desk. Sometimes he drives a blue car, sometimes he drives a gray van. I get the impression that what he drives depends on how much 'cargo' he has." She grimaced.

"Where can we find him?" Alejandro asked.

"I don't know. He might come today or tomorrow, but the few times I've seen him arrive, it's always in the afternoon. Two o'clock. Three o'clock. Around those times."

"Do other members of the staff know what they're doing upstairs?" Camila asked.

A sad smile crossed the woman's lips. "Everyone knows. It's an open secret, and we all act as if nothing is happening. We don't have much choice." Her voice dropped lower. "The administrator called me into her office one day and gave me a long speech about how valuable my services are and how much she appreciated the good job I was doing. She reminded me about patient confidentiality and asked if I had any problems carrying out my duties here. I'm certain she was testing me. I told her no, I didn't have any problem carrying out my duties. She seemed pleased and said I was eligible for a quarterly bonus. Then she ended the meeting. My bonus arrived a few days later." Tears filled her eyes.

"You did the right thing. Thank you," Camila said, taking her hand in both of hers.

Rosa took a shaky breath. "I should go now. I'll delete your information from the system. No one will know you were here, Mr. Sanchez. Good luck."

"Thank you."

After she left, the weight of what she'd told them rested in the room.

Camila turned to Alejandro with a fierce expression on her face. "They're preying on refugees and migrants, taking advantage of their desperation. These people make me sick!" she hissed.

"We'll get them," Alejandro said.

"Jandro, we have to. We have to help these people." The fierce anger of the Camila he had grown up with—the one who deeply empathized with the less fortunate and always wanted to help those in need and the marginalized in society, had risen to the surface. Nothing he did could stop her now. Job One was bringing down this operation.

"Let's see what's on the drive."

23

Back at the hotel, they used the laptop they had brought from the States to read the data Rosa had given them on the flash drive. Alejandro sat at the small desk and Camila stood over his shoulder.

The information Rosa provided was damning. She had downloaded files that included "patients" with diagnoses and medical history to justify removing their organs. The recipients' names and contact information were also logged, along with the medical staff involved in each operation. The files included five death certificates indicating death by natural causes or accidents.

Camila abruptly turned away. "I can't read anymore. I'm going to be sick."

"*Querida*—" Alejandro reached for her, but she pulled away.

"You finish looking and tell me what you find." Arms wrapped around herself, she trudged out to the balcony. It pained him to see her so upset.

Alejandro rushed through the rest of the files, which were mostly internal communications between the clinic's staff, including email threads with clients requesting specific organs.

He cursed under his breath. These people were sick. The donors were nothing to them—mere vessels to essentially be bought and sold to achieve their goals. His temples throbbed as fury built inside him at the blatant disregard for life and the obvious belief that one life mattered more than another. He wanted justice for these people.

He went outside to the balcony and slipped his arms around Camila's waist, pulling her back against his body.

"I needed some air," she said, no emotion in her voice.

He kissed the top of her head. "I understand."

For several minutes, they watched the activity on the street below.

"There's a lot of ugliness in the world," she said in a soft, sad voice.

"Yes, there is." He kissed her shoulder. "I'm going back to the clinic. I want to find The Transporter. I want to know everything he knows."

She twisted around in his arms and gazed up at him. "I'm coming with you."

"You're sure?"

"Yes, I can handle it. When this is all over, I'm writing a helluva an article—not for *Sin City Pulse* though. The topic would be too much for our magazine."

He let out a short laugh. "I agree. A different paper would be best."

"Definitely." She rested her forehead against his chest. "I'm sorry. I feel like I dragged you into a messy situation."

"Hey." He placed a hand under her chin and forced her to meet his gaze. He brushed his thumb along her lush lower lip. "Where you go, I go. And I am just as angry as you are. I want these guys. I can taste it. And we're going to get them."

The telephone in the room rang, and he went inside to answer it. "Hello?"

"Sanchez, it's me, Buck. I have some free time and wanted to see what you were up to."

His attention drifted to Camila, who looked down at the street with her arms folded on the railing. "Rosa was a wealth of information. There's a guy called The Transporter who brings the donors to the clinic. According to Rosa, he should be there this afternoon. We're going back to stake out the clinic."

"Mind if I tag along?"

"Not at all."

"I'll be there shortly."

ALEJANDRO PARKED the Honda down the street from Oasis de Vida, in the parking lot of one of the restaurants. They faced the facility, able to see cars as they entered and exited. They didn't have a detailed description of The Transporter's vehicle, but they knew what he looked like, which was helpful. Being a pale-skinned Anglo should make him easy to spot in this community.

After more than two hours of sitting in the car, talking about everything and anything, he began to wonder if they were wasting their time. Rosa had said The Transporter might come today or tomorrow, though he'd hoped for today.

"He might not be coming today," Buck said, as if reading his mind. He sat in the back seat.

Alejandro checked the time. After four. "We'll wait until five o'clock, and if he doesn't show, then we'll leave."

"I hope he shows," Camila said.

Minutes later, a little boy approached the car in cut off shorts and a dirt-stained shirt. He knocked on Camila's window and outstretched his hand using puppy dog eyes.

"Oh, poor thing," she murmured. She dug in her purse and pulled out a couple of U.S. bills since U.S. currency was widely accepted in Tijuana. Rolling down the window, she handed him the dollars. "There you go."

The boy's eyes brightened. "*Gracias, señorita*," he said happily, smiling at her with stained teeth.

He ran across the street and jetted down a pathway between the car wash and a *taqueria*.

"He reminds me of when I was a kid and me and Mamita didn't have much. Those first few years after I moved in with her, I'm pretty sure she went to bed hungry some nights to make sure I had food to eat." His chest hurt knowing the sacrifices his grandmother made to care for him after his father's death.

"That's what parents do," Camila said.

"She had already raised my mother. She shouldn't have had to raise me too."

Camila placed a hand on his thigh, and he covered her hand. "I bet she'd do it again because she loves you. And hey, you take very good care of her."

Of that, he was proud. Because of the work he had done with the Plan B organization and the money he made, he had built Mamita a nice home and deposited a stipend into her account every month to make her senior years more comfortable.

"She deserves it," he said.

The words had barely left his mouth when a blue car slowed upon approach to the clinic. The three of them straightened, and the mood in the car shifted to alert and curious.

The vehicle turned onto the property and headed toward the back. A Caucasian male with black hair and pale skin was behind the wheel.

"That might be our guy," Alejandro said.

"No one in the car with him. Maybe no delivery today," Buck mused.

"Or they're in the trunk," Alejandro said in a grim tone.

"I wouldn't put it past those assholes to do something like that," Camila muttered.

"Hopefully, he won't stay at the clinic long." The plan was to follow him to his next destination until they were able to get him alone and question him. It would be great if he went straight home, but Alejandro knew situations were seldom so tidy.

Impatiently, he tapped his thumb on the steering wheel as they waited.

"Do you think he'll be much longer?" Camila asked, shifting in the seat.

"I hope not."

No sooner had the words left his mouth than the blue sedan pulled to the edge of the curb, about to turn into traffic.

"Here we go," Alejandro said, starting the car.

The little boy from earlier came running down the sidewalk, and right away, Alejandro knew shit was about to hit the fan. The Transporter rolled down his window to talk to the boy, and seconds later swiveled his head in their direction.

"*Shiiit.* He had a goddamn lookout on the street."

Buck swore.

The man handed the little boy some money and then took off with a screech of tires.

"Hang on," Alejandro said, swinging into traffic after him.

The vehicle surged forward, almost sideswiping a Tacoma truck. The driver leaned unnecessarily long on the horn. Alejandro shot him the bird, though he was in the wrong, and kept his eyes locked on the speeding vehicle ahead.

The blue sedan weaved through the light traffic, sailed under a traffic light, and narrowly missed a pink bakery truck backing out of an alleyway.

"Bus, bus, bus!" Camila screamed, covering her eyes.

Alejandro wrenched the wheel to the left and went around

a bus with a squeal of tires that made the passengers gape at them.

"You're alive," Alejandro said, maneuvering around a taco vendor who picked that exact moment to push his cart across the street.

Camila slowly lifted her head. "This is nuts."

"I'm not letting him get away," Alejandro said in a grimly determined voice.

The storefronts shot past in a blur as they tore through the streets, winding with snakelike movement between cars at a dangerous speed. Suddenly, the blue sedan turned right down a narrow road, and Alejandro swung a hard right and followed close behind, the car tires skidding on the asphalt.

Camila whimpered, shoulders coming up to her ears as she clung to the handle above the door with a death grip.

As he flew through an intersection, Alejandro honked his horn in warning, aware of his surroundings while keeping the blue sedan in sight. They hit a stretch of road where there were less cars and open space replaced the retail establishments.

"Where is he going?" Buck asked.

"Out of the city," Alejandro said, more to himself than to answer the question.

The Transporter turned left and headed off road. In the waning light, the ground transformed from asphalt to gravel and dirt, and the sedan kicked small clouds of dust in its wake. They climbed over the crest of a small hill, and Alejandro saw the opportunity to pull up beside him since the sedan was having a much harder time navigating the terrain than the crossover.

Bouncing over the uneven road, he ate up the distance between them. Alejandro pulled alongside and intended to run him off the road, when he saw the dark muzzle of a gun through the open window of the blue sedan.

"Gun!" Camila screamed.

lejandro fell back as the weapon discharged twice. One bullet hit the body of the Honda and the other went wide.

"Get down!" he barked at Camila.

Camila doubled over and covered the back of her head with her hands. Alejandro floored the accelerator with the intention of landing a forceful hit on the right side of the sedan which, if he did it right, could destabilize the car and cause it to fishtail or even flip.

But he had two problems: the rough terrain could cause *him* to miss and damage the Honda, leaving them stranded. He also couldn't risk making such a dangerous move with Camila in the car. By himself or with Buck alone, he wouldn't have thought twice about the maneuver.

The crack of gunfire split the air, and Alejandro stayed to the right, out of the line of fire, but The Transporter leaned out the window and fired again. The round cut through the side mirror and Alejandro muttered a curse. Buck was going to kill him for damaging his car.

The Transporter leaned out the window again, and

Alejandro anticipated hearing more gunfire. Except... there was none. The man pulled his hand with the gun back in the window, apparently having run out of ammo. Perfect.

"You can sit up now. He ran out of rounds."

Camila slowly lifted her head. "Oh, thank goodness," she breathed.

"Buck, I have an idea."

Ready, Buck leaned forward. "What are you thinking?"

"I need you to take the wheel."

Camila swung her head toward him. "*Excuse me?*"

Alejandro shot a look at Buck in the rearview mirror. "We'll switch places, and I'll go out on the hood. Get me close to his car." Having worked with Buck before, he trusted him completely.

"Not a problem," Buck said, already in battle mode.

Camila, however, gawked at them. "Are the two of you serious?"

Alejandro popped off his seatbelt. "If Buck gets me close enough, I'll be able to jump onto The Transporter's car."

"*Jump onto his car?*" Camila shrieked.

"It's the only way to stop him. Anything else would be too risky."

"That's risky!" Camila yelled, eyes wide.

"Trust me, sweetheart, we know what we're doing." Alejandro maintained a safe distance between the two vehicles.

"What if Buck screws up and you die?"

"I won't screw up, and he won't die," Buck promised, releasing his belt.

Camila gripped Alejandro's arm. "Please be careful."

He brought her hand to his lips. "I don't know any other way to be."

"I'm not convinced," she said.

He pushed the seat back to provide more room, the entire

time keeping the blue sedan in sight as both vehicles bounced across the dirt road.

He undid his belt buckle.

"Why are you getting undressed?" Camila asked.

"Normally, it's hard as hell to break the window of a car, but with the right technique, it's easy. If I use a sharp object, like the corner of this belt, I can break the glass a lot easier."

"Smart," Buck said.

Worry filled Camila's eyes when she looked at him.

Alejandro squeezed her thigh. "Don't worry."

"This is what I get for wanting to come along," she muttered.

He wound the belt around his hand and then rolled down the window. Adrenaline pumped through his veins. This was the kind of shit he lived for. "You ready, *amigo*?" he asked, meeting Buck's gaze in the rearview mirror.

"Ready."

"I'll count to three and take my foot off the accelerator. Then you can take control of the vehicle."

"Roger that." Buck leaned forward with a determined expression on his face.

Camila drew a shaky breath.

The tension in the vehicle grew thick.

Alejandro flicked his eyes from the road to Buck and nodded. He eased onto the window sill, keeping his foot on the gas. One hand gripped the roof for balance, while the hand with the belt held on to the left side of the steering wheel.

Buck braced a hand on the center console as he gripped the steering wheel with the other.

"One, two, three!"

As Alejandro lifted his foot off the pedal, Buck slid into the driver's seat and took control of the car. The car swagged and skidded in the dirt, but it straightened under Buck's firm hand.

"Hold her steady!" Alejandro yelled over the roar of the engine.

Grunting, he hoisted himself completely out of the vehicle, his feet firmly planted on the edge of the door as the wind howled around him.

He said a quick prayer, kissed the cross on his chain, and climbed onto the hood. In a crouched position, he held onto the edge closest to the windshield and narrowed his eyes against the dust kicking up in his face. Using his arm to protect his nose and mouth, he looked back and nodded at Buck, letting him know to move closer.

His friend slowly closed the gap between the two vehicles. Both cars bumped along the uneven dirt road, but Buck kept pace, as Alejandro knew he would.

He was about to jump when the sedan hit a particularly deep hole. The Honda followed suit, and the entire machine rattled. He gripped the hood, his body coiled and his muscles tensed.

After taking a moment to get settled, he caught sight of Camila's wide-eyed, worried expression. He waved for Buck to move closer again. He moved slightly to the left and gunned the engine. With the surge, he edged the white vehicle alongside the blue sedan.

Now was the time.

Alejandro let go and launched himself across the small gap between the two vehicles and onto the roof, right as The Transporter veered away.

The jolt made him slide on the smooth surface, but he grabbed the edge of the roof and held on tight with gritted teeth. The car shifted left then right as the driver tried to shake him. Muscles straining, he continued to grip the roof and unraveled the belt. He lifted his hand in an arc and... the sedan jerked violently as it hit a bump.

"*Mierda*," Alejandro muttered, curling his fingers to hold on.

Heart pounding, he lay low on top of the vehicle as it zigzagged along the dirt road. His body was thrown from side to side, but he held firm.

Finally, another opportunity arrived, and he swung the belt buckle in a downward arch. The pointed corner hit the edge hard where the glass was weaker, and it shattered into pieces. To take advantage of The Transporter's temporary surprise, he swung one leg inside the car. The Transporter reached across to push him out, but Alejandro got the upper hand and kicked him in the head.

The vehicle jerked to the left and then right. While the driver fought to straighten the car, Alejandro slid the rest of his body inside and onto the glass-covered passenger seat.

The Transporter threw a punch, but Alejandro caught it and slammed his fist into the man's side. He howled in pain. He hit him again with a brain-jostling blow to the temple, and the driver lost his grip on the steering wheel.

"Stop the car!" Alejandro yelled.

The Transporter grunted and Alejandro hit him again. His head slammed into the window and blood flew from his mouth onto the steering wheel.

The sedan jerked violently as The Transporter's hands slipped from the wheel, and the car skidded off the road. They crashed through the brush and rolled into a ditch. The vehicle teetered on two tires before collapsing onto its side. Alejandro tumbled to the ground through the broken out window, while The Transporter's seatbelt held him trapped in the seat.

Alejandro took a moment to shake off the temporary dizzying effects of the crash and then crawled into the backseat and out the back door. He opened the driver's door and unhooked The Transporter's seatbelt, dragging him from the vehicle to the sound of protesting moans. The man was dazed, with a bloodied and reddened face from the blows Alejandro had landed.

Camila and Buck ran over and looked down at them. "Are you okay?" she asked anxiously.

"Better than this guy." He hauled the driver up the incline by his arm.

"Great job," Buck said with a grin.

Camila was not as complimentary. "You almost gave me a heart attack," she said, an undercurrent of anger in her voice.

With a satisfied grin, Alejandro shoved The Transporter toward the waiting Honda. "But I didn't. We have our guy. And no one died."

25

The Transporter, whose name Camila had learned was Clinton, was tied to a folding chair in the empty room of an abandoned house Buck directed them to after the chase. He and Alejandro stood in front of Clinton—both men intimidating in size, glaring down at him with arms crossed.

They couldn't look more different. Alejandro, with his dark hair, swarthy skin, beard, and dark dust-covered clothes, contrasted sharply with Buck's blond hair, beardless face, and a pristine white T-shirt and jeans.

Camila watched Buck with renewed interest. With his physique and rigid jawline, he appeared as menacing as Alejandro. No way he only drove a taxi.

"Are you going to kill me?" Clinton asked. He was American and tried to sound brave, but she heard the tremor in his voice.

"We haven't decided yet," Buck answered.

Camila stood behind them in the shadows and out of the way. Her senses buzzed from the car chase. Underneath the excitement, she was a little turned on by Alejandro's strength, determination, and skills.

The past few days during which he had killed the men in her apartment and captured Clinton showed how dangerous an opponent he could be. She couldn't wait to climb on top of him and ride him to heaven tonight. Her nipples peaked at the very thought. He'd turned her into a horny little slut, she thought with amusement.

"I don't know nothing," Clinton said.

Alejandro turned to Buck. "A double negative. Help me out, but doesn't a double negative in English become a positive?"

"You're correct, it does. Which means he *does* know something."

Both men returned their attention to their captive.

"You're going to tell us everything you know about the organ harvesting taking place at Oasis de Vida, or we're going to take out your kidney and donate it to a deserving patient." Buck removed a switchblade from his pocket and flicked it open.

Oh crap. Camila held her breath.

"You're nuts," Clinton accused, his attention hopping between both men.

"Sounds fair," Alejandro said to Buck before turning to Clinton. "Unless of course, he cares to talk."

Clinton frowned, obviously unable to decide if they were kidding or not. Camila couldn't either. Were they joking, or were they really willing to cut him open?

Buck shrugged and moved towards Clinton.

"Wait! Wait!" His eyes stretched wider, and he scooted back in the chair. "I'll tell you what I know, but you have to understand, I'm a small part of this operation. I'm a transporter, that's it. Are you law enforcement? Who are you?"

"We will ask the questions," Alejandro said, his harsh tone brooking no argument. "Where do you find the organ donors?"

The man swallowed hard, his Adam's apple bobbing up and down. "Everywhere."

"What does that mean?"

"I don't know all the details, but some people are recruited online. Others are found in person. We—*they*— have people planted in agencies providing government assistance. They refer those clients to us, and the people in charge make them an offer. Listen, the truth is, half these people don't fully understand what they're getting themselves into. If they're uneducated, it's easy to tell them a lie about what's going to happen to them."

"For example?" Buck prompted.

The man licked his lips and gave a negligent shrug. "Some of them believe they have three kidneys or think their kidneys will grow back. They don't know any better." He laughed, but when no one else joined in, he stopped and straightened in the chair. "When they get paid, the surgery or loss of a body part doesn't matter. They receive as little as five hundred U.S. dollars, but it's a lot for these people."

"We were told some of them are migrants or refugees," Alejandro said.

He nodded. "Sure, we approach them too. They're probably the best ones because they're more desperate. For instance, if they're traveling to the United States but don't have the money to pay a smuggler, an organ could pay the fee."

"So you have connections or a relationship with the smugglers."

He nodded. "There's a lot of money to be made."

The callous indifference with which he spoke about his human cargo was disturbing.

"Are any of these people *forced* to give up their organs?" Camila asked.

Clinton grimaced, shifting in the chair. "Not everyone is a willing participant. As demand has increased, some of the migrants are kidnapped and coerced into giving up their organs."

Camila had suspected as much, but hearing him admit to such a heinous act made her sick to her stomach.

"How often are donors killed?" Alejandro asked.

The man dropped his eyes.

Buck kicked the chair leg. "Answer the question!"

"I don't know!" Clinton's face turned green, as if he was about to throw up. "I'm not saying what they're doing is right, but... I know some of them are killed. Not all organs can be harvested and the donor kept alive afterward. There have been times when I've transported a donor to the clinic, and I never saw them again." His explanation matched what Rosa had said.

"Isn't it possible one of the other drivers took them?" Buck asked.

Clinton slowly shook his head. "No. Whenever we pick up a donor, we also drop them off. Each driver has a log, to keep the inventory straight, so there's no confusion. When a donor isn't going to... to... to leave the hospital... they let me know about those situations, and I adjust my sheet."

Camila and Alejandro had already known this bit of information thanks to Rosa, and the death certificates provided proof. Hearing how much they devalued the lives of the poor and less fortunate was shockingly horrible.

Clinton continued, his eyes pleading for understanding. "I don't agree with—with killing people, but it is what it is. But the others, like the kidney donors, what's so wrong about that? Someone might need passage into the country or money for God knows what, and they're willing to give up a kidney in exchange for money. So what? So what if someone has the financial means to purchase the organ? You think you're any different than those people? How would you feel if you had to be on dialysis for five, six, seven years? Huh? Then you find out you could buy a perfectly good kidney and live comfortably again and not have to worry about dying. It's a trade. That's all.

Buying and selling goods. It's *their* body. They should be able to do what they want. Everybody wins!"

Although he was right—it was their body—his sales pitch didn't change Camila's mind.

Alejandro slowly clapped as he took two steps closer to the bound man. He glowered down at him. "You really think you did something with your little speech. You are a real piece of shit. What you said would sound a little better if you hadn't admitted to telling lies to convince some of these people to go under the knife. And let's be honest, the ones donating the organs aren't making the real money, are they? Five hundred dollars? A couple thousand at best? Then you get your cut and the doctors get theirs, of payments that can reach hundreds of thousands of dollars. If this is such a great idea, why lie to the organ donors? Why not tell them the truth about how many kidneys they have? Why not give them their fair share? You try to make what you do sound altruistic, but the truth is, you're human poachers, preying on the poor and vulnerable."

Clinton's face turned red as a cherry and dropped his gaze.

"Look at me!" Alejandro said, his body tense with anger. "We want your contacts. We want to know everywhere you have recruits. This operation is getting shut down. If you cooperate, maybe you won't spend the rest of your life in prison for illegal organ harvesting and as an accessory to multiple murders. Are we clear?"

"Clear," Clinton said in a low voice.

T he raid on Oasis de Vida took place in the evening of the next day. Alejandro, Camila, and Buck were in a restaurant nearby when a line of police vehicles arrived with flashing red and blue lights.

"Here we go," Buck said.

They quickly paid for their unfinished meals and went outside to watch from a distance.

Because of the cross-border implications, agencies on both the U.S. and Mexican sides were working together. Camila stood in front of Alejandro, elated as she watched the officers descend from their vehicles and block the exit from and entrance to the back of the building. Soon after, a federal police unit with Policía Federal on their hats arrived, followed immediately by two dark SUVs. When the occupants descended, they wore blue FBI windbreakers.

With so much commotion, bystanders congregated on the sidewalks, everyone asking what was going on and pulling out their phones to capture the unfolding scene. Employees were marched out of the building in handcuffs, ducking their heads to hide their faces. One doctor came out wearing blood-stained scrubs and a surgical cap, as if they had interrupted him in the middle of an operation. He at least had the grace to appear shame-faced with a bent head.

The speed with which the government organizations had coordinated to close the clinic demonstrated how seriously the authorities took the crime. Their intention was to shut down the network right away. She looked forward to when the prosecutions began.

They stayed until the local press arrived, and then they slipped away, walking several blocks to where Buck had parked his taxi. They climbed in the car, and he took off.

Camila twisted around in the seat to look at Alejandro. "Hopefully, there'll be enough evidence there to not only arrest Dr. Shapiro but Javier Reyes too."

"We hope," Alejandro said.

"You're doubtful?"

"Men like Reyes know how to cover their tracks. He's been involved in shady business for a while."

"I'll keep my fingers crossed he's implicated," Camila said. She twisted back around to face the front, refusing to lose the triumphant energy coursing through her veins.

When they pulled up in front of the hotel, Buck stepped out and shook Alejandro's hand. "It was good seeing you again, my friend."

"Likewise. I appreciate your help."

"Anytime. It was very nice to meet you, Camila. Hopefully, we'll see each other again, under different circumstances."

She gave him a hug. "I hope so too, and maybe you'll even tell me the truth about what you really do for a living, since it's clear you're not a taxi driver."

His blue eyes lit up as he laughed. "Until next time," he said, refusing to respond to her comment.

They waved goodbye and waited outside until he drove off.

Upstairs, Alejandro and Camila went onto the balcony and watched the activity of the street below.

"How about we stay an extra day and go to the beach?" Camila suggested.

"Great minds do think alike, because I was going to suggest we stay longer. There will be less crowds at the beach this time of the year."

Camila reached for his hand. "Thank you so much for your help. I couldn't have done this without you. Not only did we get justice for Doug, those immigrants and other people will have justice too. I hope they throw the book at those bastards, and I can't wait until they take down Reyes."

Seated in the dark of his den at his compound outside Las Vegas, Javier Reyes sipped his cognac as he stared through the window.

When he received the call from one of his men about the bust in Tijuana, he had not only been surprised, he'd been furious.

He watched a brief video on his phone, put together by the local news and sent to him by one of his men. The entire time his insides churned with anger. The news had descended like a pack of wolves, reporters shouting questions to accused staff as officers marched them out the building. Inventory bags, boxes, and computer equipment were all removed from the site and packed into vans.

The scene seemed chaotic, but an audible gasp went up from the crowd of onlookers when two bodies, covered in sheets, were removed from the premises and loaded into the waiting medical examiner's van. Javier turned off the video then. He'd seen enough.

He switched his phone to look at the other interesting piece of media his man had sent—a close-up photo of the bystanders. To say he was shocked to see Alejandro and Camila standing in the crowd was an understatement. He had no proof, but they were the reason for the authorities swooping in to make arrests and dismantle his multi-million dollar network. Otherwise, why were they in Tijuana? They were both of Mexican descent, but seeing them outside the clinic was too coincidental.

He sipped his liquor, his mind running through the different ways to eliminate the problem of Camila Hughes and Alejandro Sanchez. They had turned into more than a nuisance. Six years. Those two had managed to destroy *six years* of work.

His connection to the clinic was weak. David had been the face of the facility and Javier's ownership was hidden behind multiple layers of LLCs. At the end of the day, there was nothing to tie him to the facility, and if they did somehow dig deep enough to make a connection to him, he could simply deny having any knowledge of what was taking place. Which meant he had another problem to eliminate: Dr. David Shapiro, his longtime friend.

The two had always been an odd couple. David was a scholarship guy, while Javier had attended schools his father bought his way into. Unfortunately, it was time for their friendship to end. Once the FBI descended on David, he would crack, even if Javier provided legal counsel for him. When he cracked, he would bring down Javier, and he couldn't afford to let that happen.

Unlike other people, he didn't experience remorse about what he was about to do. He had a problem that needed to be solved, and he'd solve it. No different than when he'd solved the problem of his father's betrayal, when he learned he really and truly planned to pass over him and give control of the casinos to his second in command.

He got what he deserved. He was nothing like Javier's dearly departed mother, a woman whose love and care he had always appreciated, especially since his father had treated him like an unwanted cold sore all his life.

Javier spun around in the chair and placed his drink on the desk. Picking up one of his phones, he dialed the number to a dependable person who would help him sort out how to eliminate the problems before the rest of his business dealings were jeopardized.

"Hello, Javier," the woman on the other line said. Her voice was like a purr and after all this time still shot electricity to his groin.

"Hello, sweetheart. I have a problem."

"I've heard."

Of course she already knew but listened to him go into detail and discuss the ramifications of discovery.

"How soon would you like to have these problems eliminated?"

"Immediately. What do you think?"

There was a pause. Then he practically heard her smile.

"I have an idea."

27

After a simple breakfast of coffee and *pan dulce*, Camila and Alejandro returned to their room to pack. As Camila was putting her toothpaste in her toiletry bag, she reminisced about the day before.

They had spent most of Thursday at the beach and then went to the village of Puerto Nuevo, a world famous location known as Lobster Town. With a beachside view, they ate halved lobsters served with soup, rice, beans, and warm tortillas while being serenaded by mariachis.

She wished they could have spent more time in Mexico, but she needed to return to Las Vegas. She had promised her boss at the magazine that she would return today. He wanted her to attend the Food Truck Festival and report on the diversity of food available and the rise in food trucks across the city.

She heard Alejandro moving around in the room as he packed his own bag and wondered what his plans were. Since Shapiro and Reyes's evil empire was about to crumble, when would he be leaving, and when would they see each other again?

After they finished packing, they called a taxi to take them to the airport. They mostly had an uneventful flight, choosing to avoid talking about the raid at the clinic.

When they arrived in Las Vegas, Alejandro picked up the car and drove them to her parents' house. She hadn't arranged for anyone to clean up the blood at her house yet, and Alejandro insisted they stay at her parents' place since her home was more than likely under surveillance.

They entered the house, flipping on lights as they went. Upstairs in the bedroom, Camila placed her suitcase at the foot of the bed and sat on the mattress, too tired to do anything else.

"Are you hungry? I'm starving," Alejandro said.

"I could eat. We should have stopped to get food on the way from the airport."

He nodded his agreement. "I'm craving the soul food you bought the other day."

"Mmm, me too," she admitted.

"Do you want to head over there?"

She groaned. "Do you mind going without me? I'm bushed."

Alejandro walked over and kissed the corner of her eye, then her cheek, then her lips. "I can do that for you. What do you want?"

"Same as last time."

"All right. I might try something different." He kissed her again and headed toward the door.

"The meatloaf is good. So is the fried chicken," Camila called after him.

"Maybe I'll get both."

She smiled, knowing he had the appetite to eat both meals. She plopped onto her back and stared up at the ceiling, listening to the garage door open and close as he left.

Spending time with Alejandro was so different than spending time with Emilio. They had been content, for lack of a better word. With Alejandro, she was more than content. She was euphoric, and the sex–well, the sex was toe-curling good with a rawness she hadn't experienced before. The difference between settling for 'good enough' versus being with the man you loved.

She dragged her body off the bed and went to use the bathroom. When she came back out, her phone beeped from a notification coming through. With a quick glance, she saw a short text on the screen from the owner of the magazine: *Sad news.* The text included a link, which she clicked.

Disbelief crashed over her. Stunned, she blinked—once, twice—hoping she had misread the article, "Beloved Local Clinic Doctor Found Dead in His Home."

As she continued reading, a freezing chill snaked down her spine. Dr. Shapiro was dead.

His wife had been the one to find his body in their home after returning from a trip to New York. According to police on the scene, Kathleen Shapiro had been hysterical.

Camila's hand covered her mouth. Poor Kathleen. What a shock discovering her husband's body must have been.

She quickly dialed Alejandro's number.

"I already put in the order, so if you changed your mind, you're out of luck," he said upon answering.

"I didn't call about the food. Alejandro, you're not going to believe this." She told him about the article and finished with, "He killed Dr. Shapiro so he wouldn't talk and implicate him. It has to be him, and he'll walk away from the consequences."

"I was worried something like this would happen. Men like Javier Reyes don't go down easily," Alejandro said in a grim tone.

"What can we do?"

"Nothing, for now. What about the Community Care Center? Do you know if they've been raided?"

"Hang on." Camila searched and found several articles reporting the FBI had indeed been to the clinic. She read the details from one of the top stories to Alejandro. "Reyes will probably deny knowing about the illegal organ harvesting. He needs to be stopped. He can't get away with this!" Camila said angrily.

"We will figure out how to stop him," Alejandro said slowly.

The steady determination in his voice calmed her. "I know I need to settle down, but I had hoped he was caught once and for all."

"He will be, eventually. We need to see how the FBI raid plays out."

"Right."

"He will pay for his crimes, if I have to make sure of it myself."

She smiled. She didn't doubt him for one minute. "I'm going to hold you to that promise."

"Okay. I'll be there soon."

Camila hung up and took a calming breath.

As Alejandro had suggested, she should wait to see how the charges played out with the FBI investigation. There was also the collaboration between the governments of Mexico and the United States in Tijuana. Surely, between what was happening there, and the raid in Las Vegas, there was enough evidence to tie Javier Reyes to the crimes.

Of course, wealthy people never seemed to pay for their crimes. They hired the best lawyers and somehow weaseled their way out of consequences. She hoped this wouldn't be one of those times.

Her phone rang and made her jump. She didn't recognize the number. She hesitated, but on whim, answered. "Hello?"

"Camila, it's Kathleen Shapiro."

"Kathleen. Hi. How are you?"

She didn't know Kathleen well, but she'd interacted with her at the clinic on a few occasions.

"I've been better." She didn't sound good at all, as if the

weight of the world was on her shoulders. Which it very well might be, considering the developing mess surrounding her husband's businesses. "I hope you don't mind me calling. I didn't know what else to do. I don't know if you've heard, but the clinic has been raided by the FBI, and David..." Her voice cracked.

"I'm sorry. Yes, I heard about David's passing and what happened at the clinic."

"I don't know what's going on. I don't know what to do. They're saying terrible things about David and the work he did." She sniffed.

Camila didn't know what to say. "How can I help you?" she asked gently.

"I know you've done a lot of work with the homeless and volunteered at the clinic. I was wondering if I could talk to you for a bit."

"Sure. When would you like to meet?" Camila tucked her hair behind her ear.

"I could talk right now, if you're free. I'm outside."

"Outside?" Camila hadn't heard a car drive up.

"Yes."

"How did you find me?"

"Remember when you and your mother came to help at the clinic? The volunteer paperwork you filled out included this address. I hope you don't mind me popping over unannounced. With everything that's been going on, I guess I wasn't thinking."

"It's not a problem. Um... I'm just surprised."

"Do you mind if I come in, to talk for a little bit—unless you have company. I don't know who else to talk to."

"There's no one here but me. I'll be down in a minute."

Camila hung up and hurried toward the door but paused. She turned out the light, crept over to the window, and peered outside.

Kathleen was standing beside her black Mercedes in the

driveway, her short blonde hair almost iridescent in the night. Like always, she looked wealthy and well put together, tonight in a cream pantsuit and heels.

Biting her bottom lip, Camila hesitated. Kathleen was obviously alone, yet she removed the pepper spray from her purse. The few times she had met the other woman, she had never been uncomfortable around her, but with everything going on, she felt the need to take the extra precaution because Kathleen's unexpected appearance made her a little uneasy. How much did she know about the clinic's operations? Better to be safe than sorry.

Camila went downstairs and opened the door, hiding her hand with the pepper spray behind the door. "Hi, Kathleen. Come on in."

"Thank you."

Camila saw a subtle shift of Kathleen's eyes. Then she caught the quick movement of someone to her left. A man sprang from the darkness, and she swung the door to shut him out, but he wedged his foot in the way and shoved his way inside.

She whipped the pepper spray toward him, but he moved with lightning speed to snag and twist her wrist. She hissed when sharp pain shot up her arm.

"Nice try," he said in a gruff voice, which matched his appearance.

He had a full beard and dark eyes that glittered down at her with menacing intensity. He yanked her out the door, and she struggled, twisting toward him and bringing her knee up to his balls.

She didn't hit him nearly as hard as she wanted to, but it was enough to elicit a cry from his lips and force him to double over in pain. She shifted away to run but slammed into the chest of another man who had come up behind her.

She stumbled back and blindly fired a punch, which he

easily blocked. He spun her away from him and twisted her arm behind her back. Stomping on the bushes right outside the door, he shoved her hard into the wall of the house.

"Help!" she screamed.

His free hand covered her mouth, and she bit his fingers. He grunted but didn't let go of her arm.

"Hurry up before someone sees us!" Kathleen hissed.

"Fuck this," the man said.

His closed fist landed with brute force on the side of Camila's head. The blunt blow rattled her brain, and then everything went dark.

ALEJANDRO PULLED around the corner toward the house. As he approached, he saw the front door was ajar.

What the...?

He sped into the driveway, hopped out of the vehicle, and rushed into the house.

"Camila!" he bellowed.

He hoped she'd answer and demand to know why he was yelling, but deep down knew no reply was forthcoming.

Stillness was his answer.

He raced through the house, checking the rooms and calling her name. He knew it was futile but went through the motions anyway. Her purse and phone were on the bed. She wouldn't have gone anywhere without them.

He rushed downstairs to the living room. Nothing looked out of place. No sign of a struggle.

Stepping outside, his eyes searched the area and zeroed in on the trampled bushes near the door. His heart thudded out of control.

Someone had definitely been there, and they had taken Camila.

28

"Well done, darling." Javier clinked his glass against Kathleen's.

"If you want a job done, send a woman," she said with a smug smile, taking a sip of champagne.

"True," Javier said with a soft chuckle.

She went to sit on the burgundy sofa in his office at his compound, and he crossed the room and took a seat beside her. He loved his home and had worked closely with a designer to incorporate many of his own ideas, to create an escape from the hustle and bustle of Las Vegas life.

The decor of leather and dark wood gave the room a cozy feeling. It was one of his favorite rooms in the palatial home he'd built with the money he made from organ harvesting, long before he took over his father's businesses and became disgustingly rich—so rich he had been able to buy up the homes nearby so he could have the privacy he desired. He had torn most of them down but a few remained—nicer ones he considered keeping as guest quarters for when he had visitors.

Kathleen had helped him devise a plan to deal with his problems, which included getting rid of her husband. She had agreed he could be a liability based on a conversation they had moments before Javier rang.

Poor David didn't know Javier and his wife had been having an affair for years. They were kindred spirits. He considered her his partner in crime. The Bonnie to his Clyde. Having Kathleen to confide in and bounce ideas off of made life easier. She was smart and, equally important, as cutthroat as he was. The sex wasn't bad, either. Actually, the sex was phenomenal, and he looked forward to tearing the very proper looking suit off her luscious body later.

"How are things at the Pampered Princess?" she asked.

This was one of the qualities he loved about Kathleen. She always inquired about his businesses, genuinely cared about his success, and often offered ideas he could implement. She was the one who had suggested the expansion into other parts of the world, and what a brilliant idea it turned out to be. Not only were the clinics extremely successful, but having them mitigated the loss of Oasis de Vida in Tijuana.

"I talked to the general contractor about putting the more costly marble in the top floor suites. He said the change would cost another five hundred thousand in labor alone."

"As if such a paltry amount matters. Who does he think you are?"

"Exactly. I told him I don't care how much it costs, I want the marble in those rooms."

"The guests who pay a premium for those suites will expect nothing less than the best."

"Precisely what I told him." He leaned in and gave her a kiss. Her temptingly red mouth was soft. Desire tightened his loins, and he flicked his tongue across her lips.

"I appreciate you handling Ms. Hughes for me tonight."

"You're welcome, my love. I knew she would trust me. Once we found out they had landed, all we had to do was wait for the opportunity to get them alone, away from the public. When she told me Mr. Sanchez wasn't there, I was disappointed but couldn't let such a minor issue stop us from the bigger picture —bringing them to heel. If he's as smart as you think he is, he'll find the number to the burner phone I called from and reach out. Then all you have to do is—"

The ringing phone on the table caught their attention.

"Could that be Mr. Sanchez now?" she asked in a sing-song voice.

Javier put down his drink and picked up the phone. When he saw the number, he couldn't hide his glee and showed her the screen. She arched an eyebrow with a smile.

Javier answered the phone on Speaker. "Hello?"

"Where is she?" the deep voice on the other end asked.

"Excuse me, who is this?"

Kathleen shook her head at him with amusement touching her lips, as if to say, *You naughty boy.*

"You know who this is," Alejandro growled with barely contained fury.

"Ah yes, the great Alejandro Sanchez. The thorn in my side. You're quite skilled. I'd love to have you come work for me."

He knew the man would do no such thing, but he was having fun poking the bear.

"Where is she?" Alejandro asked again.

"Is that a no?" Javier experienced a ridiculous amount of pleasure from taunting him, and it was especially delicious because he had an audience. "Oh well, the offer will remain open for a few more days, to give you time to reconsider. Whatever you're making at The Cordoba Agency, I'll double it. Now, as for the 'she' in your question, I assume you're talking about Ms. Hughes?"

He examined his nails. Time for another manicure. His standing appointment at the Celestial Palace salon should be coming up soon.

"Who else do you think I'd be calling about, you piece of shit? You need to stop playing games."

"You need to stop meddling in my business."

"Leave Camila alone, and deal with me."

"Unfortunately, I can't. Your girlfriend is equally annoying and has been working side by side with you."

"Where is she, Reyes? I'm not asking you again."

Smirking, Javier shot a glance at Kathleen, who put her glass to her lips.

"Where is she? Safe and sound, locked away in a quiet room."

"There better not be one strand of hair missing from her head."

Who the hell did this guy think he was? Time to let him know who he was talking to.

Javier straightened his shoulders. "Are you threatening me? Do you have any *fucking* idea who I am? Let's get one thing straight, Mr. Sanchez, *I* make the demands and *I* determine what happens next. If you want to see Ms. Hughes again, come get her. She's at my compound, and I'm sure you know where it is. You have twenty-four hours to bring your ass here if you want to keep her alive."

"You should have never taken her. You should let her go before I get there," Alejandro said, his voice low and lethal.

Javier belted out a bark of laughter. "I have to say, you're quite the comedian. You really don't seem to understand who's in charge. I can't wait to put your head on a platter."

"You have made a terrible mistake," Alejandro said in a calm voice.

"Oh really?"

"Yes, because I'm coming for you. If I were you, I would kill myself before I get there."

The line went dead.

Javier stared at the phone for a moment. The conviction in

Alejandro's voice sent a shiver through him. Slowly, he placed the device on the table and stood.

"What's wrong? You're not worried about him, are you? He's one man." Kathleen set down her glass.

"Of course I'm not worried." Not entirely true, but he didn't want her to see weakness in him.

She walked over and caressed his chest, which normally turned him on. Unfortunately, he was distracted by the conversation.

"Javier," Kathleen said, "this is what we wanted, remember? Since we couldn't kill them at her parents' house, we lure him out here, and we kill them both here. It's cleaner, with less chance of witnesses or leaving evidence behind. Our problems will disappear immediately, and I can go back to being the grieving widow, shocked at my husband's illegal activities."

"I'm not worried, as you pointed out, because he's one man. But, I need to make sure we have enough manpower here to handle him when he comes. And we don't know when he's coming. Could be tomorrow. Could be two days from now."

"He'll come right away because he wants to save his girl-friend," Kathleen pointed out.

"True, but there's another issue. What if he calls the police?"

"They wouldn't dare step foot on your property!"

"Maybe. Maybe not. But that cocky sonofabitch, Detective Slater is looking for an excuse to give me a hard time."

"Chief Long would never allow it. He's on your side, remember?"

By 'on your side' she meant in Javier's pocket because he bribed him to avoid looking at his illegal activities.

Kathleen caressed the front of his pants. "Come to bed. Let me make you feel better."

Javier caught her hand. "You go, and I'll be up in a few minutes. I need to make a phone call."

Her mouth downturned in disappointment, but she stepped away and walked toward the door. "Don't take too long."

"I won't."

Javier rubbed his stomach. He was pretty sure the burning meant his ulcer had returned, and it was all Camila Hughes and Alejandro Sanchez's fault. He appreciated Kathleen's confidence, but he had learned not to be overly confident, no matter who the opponent. Sometimes people surprised you, and from what he'd read of Alejandro Sanchez and the organization he worked for, he was one of those people who might surprise him.

Alejandro seemed fearless and indifferent to Javier's power plays. Which meant he was capable of anything.

"We'll see who's the baddest," Javier muttered.

Retrieving his other phone from the desk, he dialed the number for his head of security.

"Yes, Mr. Reyes?"

"For the next two days, I want to beef up security here at the compound and at the casino. Extra men, more gun power, twenty-four hour service."

"Not a problem. Is there something we need to know about, sir—so we can properly assess the threat?"

Saying he was concerned about one man coming onto the property sounded silly. "These are precautionary measures. Nothing to worry about."

"Yes, sir. I'll make sure you have the additional security you need."

"Good."

Security would take care of Alejandro, and then he would be rid of both him and Camila Hughes. Life could go back to normal, as Kathleen said.

Breathing easier, he tucked the phone in his pants and left the office, anxious to continue what Kathleen had tried to start.

ALEJANDRO SAT in the dark at the house after he hung up the phone with Javier Reyes. The next number he dialed was Cruz Cordoba, the head of The Cordoba Agency.

His plan was to rescue Camila and destroy Reyes, but he'd need help, which meant calling on the people he knew he could count on. They weren't blood, but they were family nonetheless. They had been in the trenches together. The Plan B brotherhood was a small group—elite and dependable.

"Hello?" Cruz answered.

"Hey, Cruz, I've run into a problem in Las Vegas, and I need your help."

29

The next day, Alejandro opened the door, grateful for the sight of his friends and coworkers from The Cordoba Agency. "Come on in."

Because Reyes knew about the Hughes' home, Alejandro had moved to a new location. He rented two adjoining rooms at a one-star hotel on the outskirts of the city, away from the glitz and glam of the main strip.

Cruz entered first with his bags, a Cuban giant at five inches over six feet. A few months ago he'd purchased a plane for the company, which allowed them to be more nimble when time was of the essence—and time was certainly of the essence in this case.

Next came Kinsey, aka Mouse, the company's sniper. Alissa followed. She had piloted the plane from Atlanta. Her fiancé, Hossam, was right behind her. An Arab from France, he was a new employee who'd moved to Hopevale to be closer to Alissa. Raheem, their second in command and the VP of Technology, brought up the rear.

They piled their bags in a corner and then Alejandro led them through the adjacent door into the next room, where he'd shoved the desks from both rooms together to create a long work table. Getting settled would have to wait until later. They needed a plan before time ran out.

Everyone understood the gravity of the situation. Priority number one was infiltrating the compound to save Camila. The second priority was pulling together evidence to destroy Reyes's criminal empire.

"How are you holding up?" Raheem asked, setting his computer case on one of the desks.

"I'm not. I want to rip this guy to shreds." Alejandro's hands bunched into fists.

"Well, I have good news. I was able to access the property plans. Javier Reyes has a ton of acreage, but the compound itself is a smaller area made up of the house, a garden shed, a detached garage, and two guest houses used for servants' quarters."

Everyone crowded around the computer, and Raheem pulled up the details, along with satellite imagery of the grounds. They spent the next couple of hours making plans. The short notice didn't faze them. Cruz was a master planner and had organized numerous operations in the past, from extractions to gun fights. As seasoned operatives, they were prepared for various contingencies and had been subjected to tougher enemies that tested them physically and mentally. Javier and his men were no match for their small army.

Cruz pointed to an area outside the property as they reviewed the plans one final time. "We know they will have men guarding the front gate," he said in accented English. "Mouse will be positioned here to take them out, which will allow the rest of us to sneak onto the property and surprise Reyes and his men. Mouse will keep watch outside for other external threats..."

He continued talking, Alejandro listening to another solid plan unfold from Cruz's brilliant mind. Members of the team interjected with a few questions, but otherwise, the plan was set, and each of them understood their role.

They all agreed a nighttime attack was best and split up to gather supplies. Fortunately, they didn't need much. The team had brought weapons, a drone, comms, and a Wi-Fi jamming device. Now all Alejandro needed was a few items of his own.

Cruz, Raheem, and Hossam went off together, while Alejandro, Mouse, and Alissa made a couple of stops, purchasing items which included lighters Alejandro needed to make a homemade explosive device. Their trio was the first to return to the hotel room, and he immediately went to work.

"How dependable are these?" Mouse asked from her position on the bed, elbows to knees, watching him closely. Alissa stood nearby with her arms folded across her chest.

"As dependable as the real deal," Alejandro answered.

He was making flash bang devices. He considered himself an artist, and his medium happened to be explosives. In this case, he would create art with a disposable lighter which worked well as a diversionary tool.

"How does that thing work?" Alissa asked.

"First, I remove the flame shroud on the lighter, like this." He pulled apart the lighter and took out the shroud. Working quietly, he also removed the striker wheel, flint, and flint spring. Finally, he twisted the spring around the flint. "When I'm ready, all I need to do is light the flint, toss it to the ground, and boom —a big flash of light will temporarily blind the unsuspecting enemy for up to ten minutes."

He prepared several lighters and set them aside.

"Have you heard from this Reyes guy again?" Mouse asked.

Alejandro shook his head. "I don't expect to. Right now, he probably thinks he has the upper hand. I'm counting on that, anyway. He gave me twenty-four hours, which isn't a lot of time. I'm just worried he's stupid enough to try to hurt Camila anyway because he's pissed off."

"I hope he doesn't," Mouse said.

"Men like Javier Reyes are unpredictable, but if he's smart, he'll stick to the twenty-four hour ultimatum he gave me."

CAMILA WOKE UP WITH A START, her heart racing uncontrollably. She looked around wildly. She was in the same place. A dark room. Last night had not been a nightmare.

She really was handcuffed to a bed at Javier Reyes's compound. The room was stuffy and didn't contain any other furniture, and blacked out windows kept light from entering inside. All night she had been left alone with nothing to eat or drink. When she finally drifted off to sleep, she actually thought they'd forgotten about her.

This morning a man came in and gave her eggs, fruit, and juice. She recognized him as the one from the parking lot at the ME's office with the shoulder-length blond hair. Eating with one hand hadn't been easy. She considered they might have poisoned the food but was so hungry she didn't care. At least she'd die with a full stomach. He allowed her to use the adjoining bathroom and then left her alone again.

The blond returned hours later and gave her a sandwich and water. She had asked him what was going to happen to her. What did they want? Why did they have her handcuffed if the door was locked? He never answered her questions.

Her only hope was knowing Alejandro must be working on a way to rescue her from this nightmare. A nightmare of her own doing.

She had suspected something was off when Kathleen Shapiro showed up at the house, yet she had gone outside and wound up kidnapped. She mentally beat herself up. How many times had Alejandro told her to trust her instincts? If she survived, she would never doubt her instincts again.

She shifted, grimacing at the ache in her left arm, which was shackled to the bed. Anger and fear battled within her for dominance, making her heart rate skyrocket and her breathing increase.

Calm down. Calm down, Camila.

The last thing she needed to do was start hyperventilating.

She heard male voices outside the door and sat up, bracing for what was to come next. One of the men unlocked the door and entered, and light from the hall cast a beam across the floor.

"Well, well, well, I see you're awake now." He grinned.

She didn't recognize him. He was new, with dark hair. The blond remained in the hall. The dark-haired man walked over and unlocked the handcuffs, and Camila immediately massaged her wrist.

"Better?" he asked.

Did he really want credit for removing handcuffs they had put on her?

"I don't get a 'thank you'?" he asked in a mocking tone. "Come on, we're going for a walk."

"Where to?" Camila asked, her voice raspy because it was the first time she'd spoken in hours.

By way of answer, he yanked her to her feet. Camila stumbled but caught herself before she fell. That would be too embarrassing to fall in front of these men.

Her captor snapped the cuffs on both her wrists behind her back. Well, that didn't last long.

He led her outside through a side door, and she checked her surroundings. She saw nothing but bushes, dirt, and tufts of grass surrounding the property. Javier had dropped a residential dwelling in the middle of the desert, in a remote location far from the city lights. Above, stars littered the sky like scattered diamonds, and the moon's silvery glow created shadows and spotlighted the jagged outline of the mountains in the distance. A dry, gentle breeze brushed her skin, and she heard the distant wail of a coyote's call, which added to the feeling of being out in the wild.

She shivered. Partly from the coolness of the night and partly from wondering what they planned to do to her. This might be it. They might bury her out here, not unlike the burials in the numerous stories—real and fake—that began back when mobsters ruled the city.

The blond dragged her deeper into the darkness, using a flashlight to illuminate their path. The soft crunch of gravel beneath their feet broke through the silence, and her eyes followed the movement of some unknown creature as it darted into the brush ahead of them.

Her heart beat faster the farther they traveled from the main house. Camila glanced back, and saw the other man behind them. His face was cast in shadow, so she couldn't read his expression.

Normally, she enjoyed the beauty and openness of the desert, but not tonight. Not at this moment, when all she could think about was what they were going to do to her. The fresh air and organic scent of the earth and sagebrush were lost as her imagination went in a negative direction. She imagined them forcing her to her knees and executing her with a bullet to the back of the head.

She and the men climbed over a mound of sand and down the other side. They stopped in front of something out of her worst nightmare.

A hole. Approximately four feet deep. Beside the hole was an open wooden box.

Terror slithered up her esophagus, and she turned wild eyes to the blond. "You don't have to do this. Killing me will solve nothing, and you'll have a murder on your hands."

The man smiled. "We're not going to kill you."

"Then what's the box and the hole for?"

His smile widened, and then she realized what they were about to do.

She tugged on the hand holding her arm. "No! No! Please don't do this."

His grip tightened and his face turned into a determined snarl. "We have a job to do, and there was one thing Mr. Reyes told us. He wants you to be alive when we put you in the box, so you can think about what you did. If you're lucky, your boyfriend will find you. If he doesn't..." He shrugged. "Then you have plenty of time to think about how you should have minded your own business."

Her heart rate increased to a dizzying speed. Surely the rumors about Javier Reyes weren't true. This couldn't be happening. They *wouldn't* be so cruel.

"*Please.*" Camila hated begging.

She twisted free and took off running, but with her hands shackled behind her back, she couldn't get much momentum. Halfway up the mound, the blond grabbed her shirt and yanked her backward. The material cut into her throat, and with a small cry, she fell on her butt and tumbled feet over her head.

Dirty and bruised, she almost burst into tears. She couldn't, though. She had to keep fighting.

The blond approached, a furious expression on his face. "I told you—"

She fired a kick, but he caught her foot by the ankle, and slowly shook his head. "You're going to have a lot to think about."

He yanked her to her feet, and one hand clamped around the back of her neck while the other pushed her toward the hole.

Camila pushed back as much as she could, digging in her heels, but he was stronger. "Please. Don't—"

He hit her in the back of the head. She felt stinging pain

and saw a flash of light. For the second time in as many days, everything went dark.

CAMILA'S EYES FLUTTERED OPEN. Once again, she was in total darkness, groggy, and disoriented. She had a massive headache. Reaching up to touch her temple, she hit some kind of barrier.

Where am I?

Slowly, her memory came back. *No. No. No.*

She pressed both palms upward and encountered solid wood. Her eyes widened, but she saw nothing but black. She smelled soil.

No. No. No.

They had done as they promised. They had buried her alive!

Camila let out a terrified, blood-curdling scream.

30

To maintain his privacy, Javier Reyes had bought the homes around his and torn down most of them, but one—almost a mile away—turned out to be the perfect location. The two-story property was currently empty except for a few pieces of furniture left behind by the previous occupants. Raheem set up his electronics there, working in near darkness, with his drone as the eye in the sky for their nighttime maneuvers.

Thanks to their virtual recon, the team had a good lay of the land and took off on foot toward the compound. Under cover of darkness, they traveled swiftly in the shadows, dressed in all black and wearing balaclavas. They moved in single file, carrying their weapons as well as bags for retrieving information and electronics from inside Javier's home.

Nearing the compound, they split up. Mouse raced toward the nearby hillside with her sniper rifle and gear strapped to her back. Hossam, Alissa, Cruz, and Alejandro crouched in the darkness, weapons at the ready, eyes on the huge metal gate and the two men with rifles standing guard on the inside. With the glitter of the Las Vegas Strip far from their location, Javier's fortress-like mansion was mostly shadows with random pockets of light.

"Are you guys in position?" Raheem's voice crackled in Alejandro's earpiece.

"In position," Cruz confirmed.

"In position," Mouse said.

"Other than the two at the gate, the drone shows six bodies guarding the perimeter. Looks like they're heavily armed."

"I'm locked in on the two guards," Mouse said. As always, her voice was calm and steady. "Tell me when."

"Let me work my magic." Moments later, Raheem's voice came through the earpiece. "The Wi-Fi signal is jammed and the security cameras are on a loop. You're all invisible. Do your thing, Mouse."

Almost immediately, one guard's head snapped back as he was blown off his feet by a silent shot. His body hit the cobblestone with a faint thud. As soon as the second guard turned to look at him in shock, pink mist burst from his head, and he also fell to the ground.

"Two down, gate is clear," Mouse said.

Alejandro kissed the cross around his neck and then shot from the darkness with Cruz, heading straight for the giant metal gate, as tall as the one at Buckingham Palace. As they approached, a soft beep indicated Raheem had opened it remotely.

They raced through and approached the double doors leading the way into the mansion, but Alejandro caught movement to his left when two guards exited from a side door. In one synchronized motion, he and Cruz raised their guns and fired at two men before they could lift their weapons. Silencers kept the sound to a minimum.

"Two down at the front," Alejandro announced.

As an extra precaution, Cruz hurried over and shot each man in the head before joining Alejandro at the front doors.

They slipped inside and swept the dimly lit foyer. No move-ment. No guards.

Breaching the interior of the mansion was a risky proposi-tion because Alejandro suspected Javier would be waiting. Except he expected Alejandro to be alone.

"Clear," Cruz said.

That was the signal for Alissa and Hossam to leave their hiding place. They slipped inside and closed the door.

Cruz signaled for Alissa and Hossam to begin the search for Camila downstairs. They moved in silence, skirting the two-story walls to eventually disappear like ghosts around a corner.

"One down on the rooftop," Mouse said.

Alejandro and Cruz headed for the staircase. Alejandro took the lead, creeping up each step with a combination of speed and caution, straining his ears to listen for approaching guards.

Reyes had taunted him and wanted him to come there with the intention of killing both him and Camila, but Alejandro's most fervent hope was that he hadn't killed her yet. The thought of losing her... He shook his head. He refused to allow his mind to go in such a disturbing direction.

At the top of the stairs, Cruz went left, and Alejandro went right to begin his search of the rooms. He pushed open the first door and quickly assessed the bedroom was empty, but as he slipped out, he came face to face with one of the guards.

Both men froze. They stared at each other, but Alejandro recovered first and fired point blank range in the man's face. Blood splattered the wall behind him and made a mess before he crumbled to the floor.

"One down, north hallway."

Without missing a beat, he dragged him into the empty room and continued the search for Camila.

The team moved stealthily through the house, calling out kills as they went. The tension was thick. With every door

Alejandro eased open, hope rose in his chest. Each time he found an empty room, those same hopes were dashed.

"This place is huge," he muttered.

"It's a labyrinth," Alissa agreed.

Hearing voices, Alejandro crept to the end of the hall and peeped around the corner. What he saw gave him hope. Two men were standing guard outside a closed door, dressed in suits and each holding a rifle.

"I might have found where they're keeping her. Two guards outside a door on the north hallway."

"I'm nearby. On my way," Cruz said.

It didn't take long for Cruz to arrive and they both agreed that now was a good time to use the flash bang device. Alejandro lit the fuse and waited the appropriate amount of time before he tossed the lighter around the corner at the men.

Both he and Cruz turned away and covered their eyes. A loud pop exploded in the hallway accompanied by a burst of light and acrid smoke. With the guards taken by surprise, Alejandro and Cruz surged forward. Alejandro shoved one man against the wall and yanked away his gun. Planting it in his mouth, he pulled the trigger and killed him with one shot. Meanwhile, Cruz snapped the other man's neck with a sharp twist.

"Two more down in the north hallway," Cruz said.

Alejandro twisted the doorknob and shoved the door. Locked.

"You come in here, you're getting shot!" a man yelled from the other side.

He and Cruz looked at each other. Why not fire through the door?

Alejandro received the answer to his silent question when Cruz touched the wood.

"Reinforced steel," they said at the same time.

At the sound of a *click* behind them, they dived to opposite sides of the hall. Live rounds pummeled the door from the muzzle of a rifle down the hall. Rolling onto his stomach, Alejandro aimed and fired. He hit the shooter in the leg, and the man collapsed to the floor with a pained groan. When he lifted his weapon to fire again, Alejandro fired first and landed a perfect headshot.

"She's in there. She has to be," he said, launching to his feet.

"Then we need to get inside." Cruz kicked the door. He kept kicking while Alejandro watched for approaching guards.

The structure was no match for the Cuban's brute strength. Finally, the surrounding wood splintered, and when Cruz kicked again, the door popped open and slammed against the inside wall.

As shots fired from the inside, both men spun away to take cover on either side of the door.

"Come in here, and you're dead!" the shooter yelled.

"You might as well give up, because we're coming in." Alejandro took a quick peek inside, but gunfire forced him to slide to the outside of the door to avoid getting hit. Nonetheless, he caught a good view of the interior.

Javier and a woman who looked suspiciously like Kathleen Shapiro were hiding behind a desk. A guard holding a handgun stood between them and the door. Where the hell was Camila?

Alejandro signaled to Cruz with his fingers and let him know there were three people inside and one with a gun.

"Is that you, Mr. Sanchez? How dare you come into my house!" Javier bellowed, sounding like an angry bull.

"You invited me, remember? I came for my woman. Where is she, Reyes?" Alejandro checked his gun clip and pulled out another flash bang.

Javier laughed. "Did you really think rescuing her would be that easy?"

"You told me she'd be here, I expect her to be here."

"Well, she's not here. Now what?"

This man was playing games, and Alejandro was not in the mood for games.

"I'm going to give you until the count of three, and then I'm coming in." Alejandro made eye contact with Cruz as he lit the second improvised flash bang device.

"Kill him!" Javier commanded his guard.

"One, two, three." Alejandro counted fast and tossed in the stun grenade.

Another loud pop and disorienting flash of light.

They charged into the room. Cruz grabbed the guard and tossed him to the floor before he put a bullet in his temple. Alejandro hopped over the desk, grabbed Javier by the back of his collar, and shoved him into the middle of the room.

The billionaire stumbled backward and collided with a chair, crashing to the ground when both he and the chair toppled over.

Alejandro touched his cold gun to the woman's head. "Don't move."

Eyes still closed from the effects of the flash bang, she whimpered and slunk down to the floor.

Javier pushed onto all fours. His breathing was ragged as he squinted up at Alejandro.

Alejandro ripped off his balaclava. He wanted Javier to see his face and know for sure Alejandro Sanchez was the one standing before him. "It's over. Tell me where she is."

31

Quiet and deadly, Cruz walked up and looked down at Javier with the same disgust Alejandro felt.

"You better tell him where she is. I can't stop him from killing when he's like this," he said.

"I'm not telling you anything!" Javier exclaimed.

He sounded like a petulant child, scooting backward on the carpet as Alejandro stalked him with slow steps.

"I'm going to count to three, and you better give me an answer." He released the safety on his gun and pointed the muzzle at Javier.

"You're not going to kill me. If you kill me, you'll never find out where she is."

Alejandro bared his teeth like a jackal. "I don't plan to kill you. I will just put holes in you until you tell me what I need to know. Let's do another countdown. One."

The other man's eyes widened. "You wouldn't dare."

"Two."

"Wait a minute, wait—" His voice shook.

"Three." Alejandro pulled the trigger and released a round into Javier's shin.

He let out a high-pitched scream and clutched his injured limb as his face contorted in agony.

"Let's try this again." Alejandro's voice was calm and measured. "I'm going to count to three, and if you do not tell me where she is, I'm going to put another hole in you."

"Okay, okay, wait, wait—"

"One."

"Wait!" Javier screeched, not at all sounding like the in-control wealthy businessman from their previous conversation. He gulped. "I don't know where she is."

Alejandro cocked his head in disbelief. "What do you mean you don't know where she is?"

"I have an idea, but I don't know exactly where. I had my men take care of her."

"Where. Is. She?" Alejandro's patience was wearing thin. He was itching to put a bullet in this man's head, and the only reason he hadn't was because he needed to find Camila.

"If you killed all my security, then finding her will be a tad bit difficult."

"Still playing games, Reyes?"

"I'm not." Sweat broke out on his upper lip and blood from the wound soaked through his pants.

"If I have to search every room in this house, I will."

"That's the thing—she's not in a room. She's not in the house."

"Then where is she?" Alejandro yelled.

"Tell him!" Kathleen screamed.

Javier smirked. "I had them bury her. In a box. She's probably already dead. She's been down there three, maybe four hours already."

"What did you say?" Alejandro asked.

The billionaire looked up with blatant defiance. "They buried her."

Cruz's body stilled, and Alejandro's blood ran cold. Maybe

he had misunderstood. "Where?" He didn't recognize the choked sound of his own voice.

"Somewhere on the back of the property. They buried her alive."

Alejandro's knees almost gave way.

Buried her alive. Buried her alive. The words repeated in his head like a torturous echo.

He stormed over to Javier, who shrunk back like the coward he was. Alejandro shoved the muzzle of the gun to the middle of his forehead, his finger itching to squeeze the trigger.

"Where is she, you son of a bitch? Where on the property? *Where*?" he roared.

"I-I don't know exactly. If you killed all my men, that's all I can tell you."

"Is everyone dead?" Cruz asked.

"We took out all the security. Inside and outside," Alissa said.

The world was spinning out of control. This couldn't be happening. Being good at their job had actually backfired.

"Raheem, how good is that drone at detecting heat below the surface?" Alejandro asked.

"Negative. It's not that type of drone. But I can send it over the property to search for areas where the earth looks disturbed."

"Do it," Alejandro said.

"Done."

Alejandro turned to Javier. "You better pray she lives, or I'm going to take my time torturing you until you'll wish you were dead." He shot Javier in the thigh.

He cried out and rolled onto his side, clutching his wounded leg.

"I'm going to find her," Alejandro said to Cruz.

"Go. I'll take care of these two."

Alejandro sprinted out the door and dashed toward the staircase. He didn't want to waste another second.

ALEJANDRO NEEDED A SHOVEL, so he was on his way to get a shovel. He burst into the garden shed and pulled one off the wall.

"I'm coming with you." Hossam blocked the doorway. He had removed his mask.

"Then you'll need this." Alejandro tossed him the shovel and grabbed a second one off the wall.

"Raheem, what do you have?" he asked, racing toward the back of the property.

"I'm looking. Nothing yet."

"Give me something." His voice sounded strained, and the pain in his chest hurt something awful, as if someone had crushed his heart under the heel of a boot. Fear was eating him alive. He couldn't lose Camila.

With the drone overhead, he and Hossam moved across the uneven terrain, searching in the dim light for unusual patches of earth on the property.

Suddenly, Mouse ran up. She had a flashlight with her, and without a word, she joined the search. Time slowed to a crawl. Several times, Alejandro went over an area twice to make sure he didn't miss the possibility of finding Camila. Each time he was crushed by almost debilitating disappointment.

"I see something! On the other side of the mound, fifty feet in front of you," Raheem said.

A possibility!

The three of them raced over the top of the mound, Alejandro's heart bumping against his chest. He had to get to her in time. It couldn't be too late.

On the other side, he skidded to a stop.

"*Jesús Cristo.*" He stared in disbelief at the barely noticeable patch of disturbed dirt. Javier's men had done such a good job of blending the grave with the rest of the area, it was very possible they would have missed this spot.

"Well...?" Raheem asked.

"I think this is it," Alejandro replied.

He and Hossam immediately started digging. If those bastards put her six feet under, digging her out could take at least four hours. They'd have to work in shifts.

Over and over, Alejandro shoved the blade into the earth and heaved dirt to the side. After a while, his chest hurt with the effort, and sweat glistened on his skin despite the cool night air drifting over him.

Still, he dug deeper, pausing for a second to wipe the sweat from his brow before continuing to scoop and toss dirt. The landscape around them was eerily silent. All he heard was the cut of the shovels each time they sliced through the soil, and the subsequent grunt he and Hossam made as they lifted them out.

When Hossam paused to take a breather, Mouse took his place but Alejandro continued working. His muscles ached, yet he couldn't stop. His woman was down there, and he had to save her. He hoped she had enough air to last the number of hours she had been buried, but so much could go wrong. If the box was buried deep, the weight of the dirt could cause the box to buckle and collapse on top of her. Or if she panicked and started hyperventilating, she'd lose oxygen faster and go into cardiac arrest.

From the corner of his eye, he saw Cruz, Alissa, and Raheem approach. All three had removed their balaclavas and moved like shadows in their all black outfits.

"Do you need a break?" Cruz asked.

Panting, Mouse looked up. "I do."

Cruz took her place and hopped in the hole with Alejandro.

"Alejandro?" Raheem asked.

"No."

He didn't know how long he'd been digging. An hour? An hour and a half? Didn't matter. He was not going to stop.

The blade of his shovel hit something hard and unyielding. He and Cruz exchanged a look. The hole was not as deep as he thought. Energized by a surge of adrenaline, Alejandro shoveled faster, tossing the dirt into heaping, messy piles.

"*Ya voy. Ya voy*, Xochitl," he whispered.

When they uncovered a simple wooden box, Alejandro dropped to his knees and frantically scraped off the dirt with his bare hands.

Mouse shined the light over the cover. It was nailed shut, with one nail on each side.

Cruz climbed out of the hole, and Alejandro braced his feet in the dirt on either side. He hovered above the makeshift coffin and pulled. It didn't budge. He pulled again, groaning, his muscles bunching as they tightened under the strain. The lid gave a little.

He let go and then pulled again, yanking harder, using as much power as he could.

"Come on," Mouse whispered.

A crackling sound filled the air as Alejandro tore the lid from the box. He released a roar of triumph, yanked the top all the way off, and pitched it to the side. Then he stared down in dismay at the love of his life. Eyes closed, body still.

He lifted her from the wooden box and climbed out of the hole with her in his arms. He carefully placed her on the ground and checked her pulse. It was faint. He placed his ear to her nose. She wasn't breathing. She was unconscious, unresponsive, on the verge of death after being deprived of oxygen.

He began rescue breathing to force air into her lungs. Alissa took off running, but Alejandro barely registered that she'd left. The others remained in place, supportive in their silence.

Lifting Camila's chin, he tilted back her head to open her airway. Pinching her nose closed, he covered her lips with his, and then blew into her mouth, at the same time checking to see if her chest rose.

It did!

Mouse let out a gasp. She saw the movement too.

He blew in another breath, taking his time and careful not to be too forceful. Every five seconds, he breathed into her mouth.

Suddenly, she started coughing and took huge gulps of air as her lungs worked again. Her breaths were fast and harsh. Her eyes fluttered open. He saw the confusion and disorientation in her expression.

Murmurs of relief went up from his colleagues.

"I'm here, *querida*," he whispered, watching her carefully.

"Ale...?" her voice sounded weak, and she coughed again.

Alejandro cradled her against his chest. "It's okay. I have you. I have you." His voice was thick, and tears of relief sprang to his eyes.

"Wh-what happened...?"

She was disoriented, her brain filled with fog.

"We are going to the hospital." Alejandro stood and lifted her in his arms. Her limbs hung loosely. She took a ragged breath as he climbed over the mound with the others right behind them.

He was thinking about taking one of Javier's cars when Alissa pulled up in a silver Lexus. Thank goodness she'd had the forethought to get one of his vehicles from the garage.

She hopped out. "This was the only one I could find the keys for." She opened the passenger side door, and Alejandro gently placed Camila in the seat and strapped her in.

"Thank you," Alejandro said.

"Good luck!" Mouse called, as Alejandro jumped in the car.

"Hurry!" Alissa added.

He pulled away, gunning toward the city. He knew his friends would take care of Reyes and Kathleen. His responsibility was to the woman beside him.

"Hang on, Camila."

"Ale..."

He took her hand.. "I have you. I have you."

He couldn't remember the last time he'd said a real prayer, but he did now, and pressed the accelerator to the floor.

32

A lejandro walked down the hospital hallway with a bouquet of red roses in his hands. A patient and two nurses turned in his direction as he passed.

"Lucky lady," the patient said.

"Damn, he's fine. Lucky lady indeed," one of the nurses murmured loud enough for him to hear.

He kept walking though the comment made him smile. He entered Camila's room and found her seated on the bed with her doctor standing before her.

"There he is," the male doctor said when Alejandro entered. Dr. Snow was dark-haired and in his mid-thirties, with a youthful face that made him appear closer to a high school student than an adult.

Camila beamed at Alejandro, her eyes lighting up—which was the best gift he could ever have. Seeing his woman safe and sound after her ordeal was a relief and filled him with inordinate gratitude.

"Are those for me?" she asked, already extending a hand.

"Of course." He handed them over and gave her a quick kiss.

"Thank you, baby."

She had arrived at the hospital with a concussion. Initially, the doctors said she could leave after twenty-four hours, but a persistent headache forced them to keep her an extra day to monitor for signs of a serious brain injury. After an improvement yesterday, they approved her for check out this morning.

"I was telling Camila what I want her to do when she leaves here, so I'm glad you arrived to make sure she adheres to my advice," Dr. Snow said.

"Don't worry, I'll make sure she does," Alejandro said.

Camila rolled her eyes at him, but he knew she'd listen to the doctor's orders.

"Rest is the most important part of ensuring a quick recovery," the doctor began, his voice grave. "No strenuous physical or mental activities, which means taking a few days off from work. I want you to rest. I can't stress that enough. If you find the headaches return, you experience dizziness or blurred vision, I want you to come see me or go to your primary care physician. Ease back into normal activities. Stay hydrated, and eat plenty of good, healthy food."

"If I do get a headache, can I take a painkiller?" Camila asked.

"Something like Tylenol is fine, but stay away from ibuprofen. Otherwise, you should be good to go."

A nurse rolled in a wheelchair for Camila, and she sat down.

"I'll see you in two weeks for a follow-up," Dr. Snow said.

"Yes, doctor," Camila said, hugging the bouquet to her chest.

The nurse pushed her through the door, with Alejandro about to follow, but the doctor touched his arm to get his attention. He handed him a business card. "This is a local therapist. I offered Camila the information, but she refused and insisted she was not having any issues. What she went through, being buried alive, is a very traumatic experience. If she's really fine, wonderful. However, she could have delayed trauma, resulting in nightmares or experiencing feelings of claustrophobia. She might want to talk to someone then, and Dr. Rice is wonderful. Even if Camila doesn't use her, I would strongly encourage her to see someone."

Alejandro examined the card. "Thank you."

"No problem. Have a good one." Dr. Snow slipped out the door ahead of him, and Alejandro hurried to catch up to Camila and the nurse.

After checkout, he pulled up in her purple car, and they headed to the house. "How are you feeling? *¿Estás bien?*"

"Yes, I'm fine, but I feel as if I've lived two lifetimes in a short period. It's crazy."

Alejandro held her hand.

She squeezed his fingers. "You saved me," she said.

"I didn't do it alone." Since he hadn't had a chance to explain everything to her before, he told her how his fellow agents had flown to Vegas on short notice to help.

"All that trouble for me?"

"*Por supuesto.* I needed you to stick around for selfish reasons. You haven't made *camarones embarazados* and *frijoles charros* for me yet."

Flinging back her head, Camila laughed, a sound filled with happiness and lots of relief. "That's a good reason. I guess I better make those dishes then."

"Once you're rested, I expect you to."

They pulled into the carport, and he walked around to her side of the car and lifted her out.

"This is not necessary," she said with a laugh.

"The doctor said no strenuous physical activity."

"I can walk, Jandro."

He ignored her arguments and let them into the house

where he placed her on the sofa. He had hired cleaners, and the faint odor of disinfectant remained in the air.

Crouching in front of her, he held her hand. "I want to ask you a question."

"Okay," she said slowly, looking a little worried by the seriousness of his tone. She placed the flowers, which she hadn't put down the entire time, beside her.

"I want us to get married right away. I do not want to waste any more time apart, but my life is in Georgia. Would you be willing—"

"Yes!" She flung her arms around him and buried her face in his neck. "Yes," she said more softly, her voice trembling.

Alejandro moved to the sofa and held her close. "I love you," he whispered.

"I love you too." She gazed up at him, her eyes liquid with tears.

He kissed her gently. They had a lot of time to make up for. He didn't want to spend another moment apart from this woman.

Her stomach growled, and they both started laughing.

"Are you hungry?" he asked, smoothing her hair back from her face.

"Starving," she admitted.

"What do you want to eat? I went shopping before I picked you up. We have steak, chicken, or I can make sandwiches...?"

"A sandwich is fine."

"One sandwich for my fiancée." He kissed her nose and went into the kitchen.

"Fiancée. I like the sound of that."

In the kitchen, he removed the bread, deli meat, and fixings to make sandwiches. As he worked, Camila turned on the television and flipped through the channels. He had just finished when she stopped on a local channel broadcasting a press conference for none other than Javier Reyes. The billionaire limped to the podium.

Camila gasped. "He's out on bail?"

Alejandro brought the sandwiches and drinks over on a tray and placed them on the table.

"Mr. Reyes, what do you say to people who think you should not have been released with such serious charges against you?"

Javier wore one of his tailored suits, this one black with a striped blue and white tie. "I say that in this country, you're innocent until proven guilty, and I look forward to my day in court."

"Is it true that you buried someone alive on your property?" another reporter yelled.

A faint smile touched his lips. "Of course not. That would be a monstrous thing to do. Let me be clear, none of these allegations are true. I knew nothing about the organ harvesting taking place at the Community Care Center. Dr. Shapiro and I were friends, and I invested money in his business purely as a result of our friendship, to help him during a time of financial need. Had I known he was involved in something so... heinous, I would have turned him in to the police myself."

"What about the accusations of bribery and rumors of evidence taken from your house which prove your involvement in other illegal acts?"

His features tightened in annoyance. "Nothing but rumors and allegations—a hatchet job orchestrated by my enemies. I'm being framed—I believe through the use of A.I. manipulation."

"He can't be serious," Camila muttered.

"I'm a respected businessman who employs thousands of people, and I contribute to the local economy. I will be vindicated in court, and when I am..." He looked directly into the camera, his voice cold and unyielding. "My enemies will suffer for trying to tear me down. Every single one of them will pay."

A man who looked like he could be his attorney placed a hand on his shoulder. "That's enough for today. Thank you." He directed Javier away from the media, who continued yelling questions at their backs.

The camera captured Detective Slater in the audience. He watched them leave with an impassive face and his arms folded over his chest. He was an asshole, but he wasn't a crooked cop. Since Alejandro learned Slater was on the right side of the law, The Cordoba Agency team had arranged an anonymous special delivery to him at the police station, which included all the data and files they had collected at the compound.

"What do you think he meant when he said his enemies will pay?" Camila's eyes were wide with fear, and the pulse at the base of her throat beat faster.

"Tough guy talk. He needs to worry about his pending charges," Alejandro answered. He pulled her into his arms. "Don't be concerned about him, okay?" He smoothed a hand down her soft hair.

She squeezed him tight but a tremor ran through her. Her heart was beating so fast, he thought it would burst through her chest. She was terrified.

He couldn't stand to see her so afraid, but more importantly, he couldn't tolerate her life being threatened. He didn't for one minute believe Reyes was bluffing. He would seek revenge on them, and Alejandro almost lost Camila once. Time to make damn sure such a close call didn't happen again.

THE BEST TIME TO strike is when the enemy least expects it. That was one of the lessons Alejandro learned as a youth. First from his gangster father, then from the training in the Plan B program.

His expertise in explosives meant not only understanding

the technical aspects of what they could do, but how and where to source the weapons he needed. He hadn't been able to do that when Javier arranged Camila's kidnapping because time was too short. But he had more time to plan and pull together his resources over the course of a few days after the press conference. With a four-hour round trip drive to a small city in Arizona, he met a reputable contact and collected everything he needed.

Now, his work was almost done. He stood before Javier Reyes, who was tied to a chair in front of the doors of his mansion. He had arrived with a security team of two at the end of the day. He hadn't replenished his full security in the days since he'd been arrested, and Alejandro knew with his guard down, this was the best time to strike. He shot Javier's guards with tranquilizers and stuffed them into the trunk of the limo. Then he put a gun to Javier's head and told him what to do.

"You'll never get away with this!" Javier snarled, rocking in the chair in a vain effort to get loose.

Alejandro almost laughed at him. He didn't seem to understand he'd met his match, and like Javier, Alejandro was equally capable of killing without remorse.

He lit a cigar with deliberate ease and took a slow drag, letting the sweet aroma of the smoke curl around him in the waning light. He savored the smell and taste of the one vice he allowed himself. As he exhaled, a sense of calm came over him. He was in control. Javier would not win. He would never hurt anyone again. Certainly not Camila.

"Men like you never learn," he said. "Even when you are in prison, you will cause problems. I like to think of myself as the problem solver."

Alejandro had placed explosives all over the house and other buildings on the property. He hadn't had a project this big in a long time, and he was semi-hard thinking about the explosions about to rip through the property and destroy Javier's pride and joy.

What made his plan so much sweeter was knowing he had timed everything perfectly. Javier would live long enough to see the destruction of his palatial home before the final blast wave ended his life.

"This is your last chance to express your regret for the life you have lived. For the people you have hurt. If you do, maybe God will show you mercy in the afterlife."

"Express my regrets for what? If you're talking about the organ harvesting, I provided a service. I *helped* people."

Alejandro wasn't shocked by his answer. He never expected him to apologize.

"*Adiós*, Javier." He started walking away.

"Where are you going? Where the fuck do you think you're going, Sanchez! Get back here! Get back here you son of a bitch!"

As soon as Alejandro walked through the tall iron gates, he pressed the detonator in his hand. A loud *boom* came from the back of the property, followed by successive *booms* blasting like thunder in the desert.

He stopped at the car he'd rented, safely out of the range of the coming blast wave. Leaning back, he crossed his feet at the ankles and watched his handiwork through narrowed eyes while he finished his cigar. Flames shot upward as C-4 charges and plastic explosives ignited and sent shockwaves through the air, lighting up the sky.

When he'd seen enough, Alejandro climbed in the car and took off for the lights of Las Vegas before the police arrived. He passed by Javier's parked limo near the foundation of a demolished house near the compound. When he arrived in town, he'd make an anonymous call and notify the police the guards were in the trunk.

Cranking up the radio, he relaxed in the seat for the drive home to his future wife.

33

A week and one day later, Alejandro was standing at the front of a wedding chapel dressed in a dark suit and a dark tie, freshly shaved with a new haircut. In the decades since it opened, this particular chapel had seen a number of celebrities get married inside, including Whoopi Goldberg, Bette Midler, and singer Barry White.

Beside Alejandro was Miguel, having returned from his honeymoon the day before. Though Alejandro had wanted to marry Camila right away, of course she wouldn't get married without her brother in attendance.

Alejandro straightened his tie and his shoulders. He wasn't nervous, just anxious to make Camila his wife. After all these years, the day he longed for but never expected had finally arrived.

Miguel leaned toward him. "I've been meaning to ask—what took you two so long?"

Alejandro pondered the question. "Life," he answered simply.

He could have said more, but there was no need. The anger he once felt when thinking about Emilio's role in keeping them apart no longer surged through him. He and Camila had both lived the lives they were supposed to live, separately. Now was their time to start a new life, together. He saw no point in dwelling on the past. He looked forward to a bright future with the woman he loved.

Patrice sat off to the side. A violinist stood at the ready for Camila's entrance, and so did a photographer provided by the chapel.

After a few minutes, the officiant entered from a side door, and a hush fell over the group. Balding, with a pair of thick glasses on his face, the older man smiled pleasantly at everyone.

"Are we all here?" he asked.

"Yes," Alejandro replied.

The double doors opened in the back via remote control and the violinist started playing. Camila appeared in the doorway, and Alejandro's chest tightened as he caught his breath.

Instead of a formal wedding dress, she wore a silk sheath dress with capped sleeves. Her hair was styled in a lovely array of curls and adorned with a white tiara. She came down the aisle carrying a bouquet of flowers with a special addition— one bright, reddish-orange flower, like the one she had given him so long ago.

When she arrived in front of him, he took her arm. "You are stunning," he whispered.

She gazed up at him, and he wanted to kiss her, but the moment would come soon enough.

"Thank you," she said.

The ceremony took approximately ten minutes, and then the official pronounced them husband and wife. Alejandro kissed Camila hard, bending her over his arm to the cheers and laughter of the attendees.

When he straightened, her cheeks were flushed and her

eyes bright. He always wanted her to be happy, and he'd do anything and everything to ensure she remained happy.

After hugs and a brief conversation, they said goodbye to Miguel and Patrice. Alejandro had booked the honeymoon suite at the Bellagio Hotel & Casino, and they rode over in a white limousine with *Just Married* emblazoned on the back window. Camila rested her head on his shoulder, and their fingers were entwined together on his thigh.

Later, in the room, Alejandro was seated on the side of the bed, buttoning his cuffs. They were going to dinner and then dancing at one of the clubs. Camila was in the bathroom.

"What are you doing in there?" he yelled. "I want to see my wife."

"Hold your horses!" she yelled back.

He had married a feisty woman. The next fifty years were going to be fun.

Finally, the door opened, and she draped one hand on the frame. She had stripped down to white lace panties and a matching bra that pushed her lovely breasts high on her chest. Her left hand rested on her hip in a sexy pose. On her head was his cowboy hat, and in the corner of her mouth an unlit cigar.

"How do I look?" she asked, her voice lowered to a husky tone that made his blood heat up.

"Come here, and I will tell you."

She came toward him with a hip-swinging walk, hands on her hips, breasts thrust forward as they temptingly bounced. She stopped in front of him. "Was I worth the wait?"

"Oh yes," he said, his eyes doing a slow tour of the delectable image she made.

"I thought you'd like this."

Alejandro took a deep breath and inhaled the sweet scent of her skin. His dick stirred from her nearness, and he reached for her, sliding his hands from the curves of her hips right up to her breasts.

"I was thinking," she said, her voice the same low and husky tone. So damn sexy. She stepped between his thighs, and his hardening erection strained the front of his pants. "We could go out tomorrow for a nice dinner. But tonight, we should stay in, order room service, make love, and then take a bath in that swimming pool size tub in the bathroom. What do you think?"

"I think my wife is a genius."

He removed the cigar from her mouth, tossed it aside, and pulled her onto the bed. She squealed as he rolled her over onto her back.

The hat rolled off her head as she gazed up at him with love in her eyes. "I can't believe this is real."

"It's real. You were sent from heaven to tame the devil," he whispered.

"No," she said, frowning and shaking her head. She cupped his jaw. "*You* were heaven sent. To keep me safe and show me what true love and happiness should be. I'm the luckiest woman alive."

"You have made me the luckiest man alive, and I cannot wait to build a life with you. Our best moments are ahead of us, *querida*."

Her smile was broad and lit up her face with raw happiness, making her pretty brown eyes sparkle.

Alejandro dipped his head and kissed her. Her lips clung to his, pillowy soft and delicious, giving way to his tongue as he sank deeper into their kiss. Sliding his hands into her panties, he slipped a finger inside her.

"You're already so wet," he groaned.

This woman had so much power over him. He kissed her neck and down the length of her body, all the way to her purple-painted toes.

Her breathless purrs were like music to his ears. "I love when you make that sound," he whispered.

He entered her with one smooth movement, and their

breaths mingled together as one, the same way their bodies joined together as one. And when she finally came, she clawed his back, trembling beneath him as she cried out his name.

LAS VEGAS during the day was much different than Las Vegas at night. As Camila drove down the strip in her purple car, she noted how much more subdued the city felt without the glitz and energy of the casinos at night.

Tourists still walked around taking photos, but the atmosphere was calmer than the night, when the bright lights transformed the strip into a loud, chaotic place buzzing with excitement.

She would miss it, no doubt—both the calm and the buzz. She'd lived here most of her life, but she was ready to move on and excited about the future with Alejandro and their new life together in Hopevale.

After Javier's compound had exploded, and she was certain she knew who did it but didn't ask, the Reyes-Shapiro scandal continued to dominate the news cycle. Kathleen Shapiro was outed as Javier Reyes's lover, and she was not only aware of her husband's organ harvesting, she was a willing participant.

She agreed to divulge more information about Javier's business dealings and illegal activities in exchange for leniency. She informed the police about the other clinics, and in a dramatic twist, she told them that Alvaro Reyes was buried on the grounds of the compound and had not gone off to live a carefree life in retirement, as so many believed. Cadaver dogs found not only his body, but the bodies of three other people who had yet to be identified.

Camila was ready to leave all the negativity behind, but she couldn't without saying goodbye to her friends at the encampment first. She parked her vehicle at the plaza like she always did and walked toward the back of the building. Her heart hurt when she thought about Doug, but at least they had achieved justice for him, and his sister finally learned the truth about his death. He had been murdered. Dr. Stenner, who was part of Reyes's organ harvesting enterprise, had lied.

Camila greeted everyone, smiling and waving and calling the ones she knew by name. When she came upon Rhonda, she lowered to her haunches.

"Hey, Rhonda."

"Hi, missy, how are you?"

"Doing pretty good. I have some news. I got married." She showed Rhonda her rings and smiled when she gasped.

"Did you marry the man from Hunks R Us?"

Camila laughed. "I sure did."

"Congratulations."

"Hot damn! Congrats," Sam said, who was seated nearby.

Rhonda's smile slowly died. "You're leaving us, aren't you?"

Camila swallowed the lump in her throat and nodded. "Yeah," she said, her voice thick.

Sam and a couple of the others quietly looked on as they listened to the conversation.

"Well, you did a good thing, getting justice for Doug and all those people."

"I hope Dr. Shapiro, Mr. Reyes, and all them people rot in hell!" Sam exclaimed.

Several others nodded their heads and grumbled their agreement.

"Where are you moving to?" Rhonda asked.

"Georgia. A place called Hopevale, right outside of Atlanta. But you'll see me again. I'm holding on to my parents' property here, so who knows... I might be back sooner than you think."

"That'll be nice," Rhonda said, her smile a little sad.

"Well, I better go. I wanted to see you all before I left."

Before she could stand, Rhonda grabbed her fingers with a trembling hand. "Take care of yourself."

The words came out in a rush, and then she quickly snatched back her hand and pulled her legs in tight to her body. Her gaze lowered and she froze, the way children do when they believe they had turned themselves invisible.

"I will," Camila said softly. She didn't want to make a big deal out of what Rhonda had done, but she was emotional nonetheless. She had reached for her. She had touched her.

Camila stood and waved, saying goodbye to the people she'd come to care deeply about. She only wished she could have done more to help them. As she returned to her car, she blinked back tears.

She *would* see them again. She would make sure of it.

34

Another wedding, but this one was different. The wedding of Hunter Miller and Sable Devereaux in the town of Hopevale had brought everyone together.

As a groomsman, Alejandro had stood beside his good friend and watched him pledge his life to the woman he loved. Neither of them had much family, but Sable's daughter had traveled from Gallaudet University to stand beside her mother as her maid of honor. Now the celebration in the event hall was in full swing.

Alejandro sat at one of the round tables with his chair turned in the direction of the dance floor, his tie loosened, and his jacket long discarded. Most of the guests were out on the floor, shaking their asses, cheering, clapping, and dancing along with the bride and groom.

Sable was gorgeous in a vintage-inspired gown and matching hair accessories, her hair pinned up in a bun. Her brown skin glowed under the lights as she danced, smiling up at her husband.

"I don't think I have ever seen Hunter smile so much," Cruz remarked. He sat in a chair on the opposite side of the table.

"Me either," Alejandro said with a laugh, sticking an unlit cigar in between his teeth.

Before coming to Hopevale, he and Camila had flown to Jalisco for a few days. He tended to his parents' graves and then they visited his grandmother. She had expressed joy and exuberant approval when she learned they had gotten married, and surprisingly so had Camila's family. Either the passing years had faded their memories of his exploits as a youth, or they no longer cared.

Alex, Cruz's almost six-year-old son, dashed toward them wearing a pair of black slacks. No shirt. No socks. No shoes. He looked like he had been in the midst of a strip tease when someone interrupted him.

Not too far behind was his mother, Shanice—a tall, thick-bodied woman with golden skin. She stalked over, an exasperated expression on her face. The little boy ran between Cruz's open legs and hid his face against his father's abdomen.

"Look at your son. I told you we should have left him at home," Shanice said. They had left their toddler daughter at home with a babysitter. "Where is your shirt, Alex?"

"I don't know," Alex mumbled against Cruz's belly. He lifted his face to his father, beseeching him to save him from his mother's wrath.

"I'll keep him here with me," Cruz said.

"He's not getting back out on the dance floor until he finds his shirt—and his shoes!" Shanice walked away, shaking her head.

Cruz looked down at his son. "Where are your clothes?"

Alex shrugged and climbed onto his father's lap.

Cruz kissed the top of his head. "Why do you give your mommy so much trouble, hmm?"

"I don't know," Alex murmured, resting his face against his father's chest.

Alejandro chuckled, as he imagined one day having a son or daughter as rambunctious and mischievous as Alex.

Tyrone Evers, who had left the police department and joined their team some time ago, approached with his wife, Ella Brooks, a woman worth billions. The couple had met when Tyrone was still on the force and investigated a break-in at her place. His sharp mind and connections with local law enforcement had proved invaluable on recent cases.

"It's getting late. We're going to head out," Tyrone said.

"You're too young to be going home already," Alejandro teased.

Tyrone chuckled. "It's the wife. You know how it is."

Ella's mouth fell open, and she cocked her head to give him an incredulous look. "Don't listen to him. He's the one who can't handle being out late. Soon as we get home, he'll probably crash for the rest of the night."

"Only because it's been a long week." Tyrone flung his arm across her shoulders and saluted with his other hand. "Good night, gentlemen. See you on Monday."

"Good night," Alejandro and Cruz said at the same time.

"Good night!" Alex yelled. He waved at the couple, and they waved back.

Mouse approached, carrying a small white shirt and miniature black shoes. "Gee, I wonder who these belong to."

"Me!" Alex said.

"Yes." Mouse turned over the shirt to Cruz. "I couldn't find his socks."

"This will at least get him back out on the dance floor," Cruz said.

Mouse crouched in front of Cruz and slipped the shoes on his son's feet. Alex then hopped down and Cruz helped him put on his shirt.

"Isn't that much better?" Cruz asked.

Alex nodded vigorously.

"Go play with the other kids, and do not take your clothes off again."

"Okay." Alex ran off.

Mouse watched him run over to where several children were dancing in a circle. "He's gonna take his clothes off again, isn't he?"

"Definitely," Cruz replied.

The three of them laughed.

"I'm going to find a server to get something else to drink. I'm parched. Can I get either of you anything?"

"No, I'm good," Cruz said.

Alejandro held up his glass of water. "I'm fine."

"Cool." Mouse lingered for a moment, as if she didn't want to leave, and then turned to walk away.

"Mouse." Cruz called out to her, and she turned back in their direction. "Are you okay?"

"Sure. Of course."

"You know what he means," Alejandro said.

Despite her lethal skills, they were all protective of Mouse because of her age. She was the youngest member of their team.

"I'm fine, really." Then she took a deep breath. "I'll be fine."

"If you need to talk..." Cruz said.

"I know. I appreciate the offer, but I'm good." She gave a smile that didn't quite reach her eyes and walked away.

Cruz and Alejandro looked at each other. The anniversary of her family's death was coming up, which was always a difficult time for her.

"I will check on her tomorrow," Alejandro told Cruz.

Later, guests gathered outside for the sendoff of the happy couple, tossing flower petals at them as they hopped into the waiting limo. Once they were gone, everyone started saying their goodbyes.

Alejandro and Camila walked hand in hand toward his vehicle and waved at Hossam and Alissa, who veered off in the opposite direction. They stopped at Alejandro's navy-blue Dodge Ram 1500 truck, and he opened the door.

Instead of climbing in, Camila turned to face him. She appeared almost angelic under the lights of the parking lot, her hair a tumble of waves past her shoulders. Large gold earrings peeked between the strands and brightened her features.

"This was a really nice wedding," she said.

"I'm happy for Hunter—for both of them."

"You have some cool friends."

He angled his head sideways. "So, what do you think about Hopevale so far, my dear wife?" he asked.

My dear wife. My wife. He hadn't completely become accustomed to saying those words. For so many years he'd been on his own, it was strange to have to check in with someone else about decisions. But he liked it. He also liked coming home to a hot meal, lying in bed together talking, watching television, or making love.

She had found a property manager who was currently working on finding a tenant for her parents' house, and in a few weeks they were going back to Las Vegas to bring all her belongings to Hopevale.

"Definitely a big change from Las Vegas," she said with a laugh.

"But you like the location?"

"Yes, I like this cute little town."

"You could live here, permanently?" He wanted to be sure. Her happiness was paramount. "We could live in Atlanta, like Katherine and Raheem, and I could commute."

"Not necessary. I'll be happy here because you're here."

Camila slipped her arms around his waist and tilted back her head to look up at him.

"Same for me. All that matters is being with you," he said. He had never said words like this to any other woman.

Her pretty eyes softened. "We're starting over. Starting fresh."

"Just the two of us," Alejandro said, cupping her face.

"Forever," Camila whispered.

"*Para siempre*," he whispered back.

Then their lips touched in a deep kiss filled with the promise of a future together—finally.

ALSO BY DELANEY DIAMOND

More books in The Cordoba Agency series!

Until Now (The Cordoba Agency #1)

For Cruz Cordoba, a simple off-the-books assignment becomes a race of life and death.

Until Death (The Cordoba Agency #2)

The best laid plans can still go awry . . . in the most terrifying way. Read the exciting conclusion to Cruz and Shanice's love story.

Heart Stealer (The Cordoba Agency #3)

Katherine was older, sophisticated, and years ago she broke Raheem's heart. Now he must keep her alive and his desire in check. Easier said than done.

Almost Perfect (The Cordoba Agency #4)

A cat burglar and an assassin run for their lives across Paris—and try not to get distracted by the sizzling attraction between them.

Forever Again (The Cordoba Agency #5)

To get a second chance at love, two assassins must survive a criminal enterprise determined to wreak havoc in America's Paradise.

Heaven Sent (The Cordoba Agency #6)

Friends become lovers as they uncover the heinous actions of an evil empire's plans.

⁓

Audiobook samples, free short stories, and the full catalogue of her books are available at www.delaneydiamond.com.

ABOUT THE AUTHOR

Delaney Diamond is the USA Today Bestselling Author of sensual, passionate romance novels. Originally from the U.S. Virgin Islands, she now lives in Atlanta, Georgia. She reads romance novels, mysteries, thrillers, and a fair amount of nonfiction. When she's not busy reading or writing, she's in the kitchen trying out new recipes, dining at one of her favorite restaurants, or traveling to an interesting locale.

Enjoy free reads on her website. Join her mailing list to get sneak peeks, notices of sale prices, and find out about new releases.

Join her mailing list
www.delaneydiamond.com

facebook.com/DelaneyDiamond
x.com/DelaneyDiamond
instagram.com/delaneydiamondbooks
pinterest.com/delaneydiamond

www.ingramcontent.com/pod-product-compliance
Lightning Source LLC
Chambersburg PA
CBHW071305250626

47159CB00004B/1312